More Praise for *Inconvenient*

"Heartfelt, honest, and brave—Margie Gelbwasser isn't afraid to uncover painful truths."

—Sarah Darer Littman, author of *Purge*

"[A] realistic, heartfelt story."

—*Kirkus Reviews*

"Gelbwasser realistically portrays the shifting emotions of a teenager navigating complicated situations and conflicting loyalties. This is a complicated drama of people sinking to the lowest common denominator and rising to their best selves to do the right thing."

—*VOYA*

"The day-to-day nature of Alyssa's story is a refreshing take on the YA problem novel, one that refuses melodrama and favors instead the powerful significance of the smaller moments of life—a smell, a look, a flash of a memory."

—*School Library Journal*

"An authentic and powerful probing of personal and family issues. Recommended."

—*AJL Newsletter*

pieces

of

us

For my grandparents, who brought me to the Catskills every summer, taught me card games and dominoes, and showed me the simpler, safer world of berry-picking. I will remember you always.

Dear Eric,

Words are power! Break the silence on bullying and abuse!

— M. Gelbwasser

pieces

of

us

Margie
Gelbwasser

f|ux™
Woodbury, Minnesota

First Edition
First Printing, 2012

Book design by Bob Gaul
Cover design by Ellen Lawson
Cover image © Fancy/Photolibrary

Flux, an imprint of Llewellyn Worldwide Ltd.

Library of Congress Cataloging-in-Publication Data
Gelbwasser, Margie.
    Pieces of us / Margie Gelbwasser.—1st ed.
       p. cm.
    Summary: Four teenagers from two families—sisters Katie and Julie and brothers Alex and Kyle—meet every summer at a lakeside community in upstate New York, where they escape their everyday lives and hide disturbing secrets.
    ISBN 978-0-7387-2164-4
    [1. Emotional problems—Fiction. 2. Family problems—Fiction. 3. Brothers and sisters—Fiction. 4. Interpersonal relations—Fiction.] I. Title.
    PZ7.G276Pi 2012
    [Fic]—dc23

                                                    2011036284

                                   Flux
                          Llewellyn Worldwide Ltd.
                           2143 Wooddale Drive
                          Woodbury, MN 55125-2989
                             www.fluxnow.com

                    Printed in the United States of America

Acknowledgments

I would like to thank Brian Farrey-Latz for his great edit ideas and for buying *Pieces of Us* before either of us knew what it would become, just because he believed in me. Steven Pomije and Courtney Colton for answering my million questions. Sandy Sullivan for her keen eye, fantastic ideas, and for always finding ways to make my manuscripts better. Everyone at Flux for letting me publish this book and for allowing me, two years ago, to start my career as a published novelist. It all means so much to me. My agent, Jennifer Laughran, for supporting all my efforts, always listening and telling me whether my concerns are valid or not. My friends and best readers, Vinessa Anthony and Shaun Hutchinson—you know how thankful I am for you both. To Alex for lending two more eyes despite being busy with twins, writing, and teaching. To Matt for his info on Philly (told you I'd thank you here). To my family for always supporting me with babysitting, love, and encouragement. To my little guy, Noah, and husband, Stu —you both keep me going, and I love you.

Katie

~The Lake House: Something to Know~

I first met Alex (or Sasha, as his grandparents call him) the day the chicken man came to the lake houses. I was nine, Sasha was eleven. I heard about the chickens all week, how some man was going to come and bring fresh ones for everyone to pick. I was really excited because I thought it meant we'd get our own chicken to feed. I asked my grandparents if we had enough food for them. They gave each other worried smiles.

The day he came, I sat on the bench closest to him. There were so many chickens. He had a little pen for them to roam in so people could see which one they liked best—which they clicked with, I thought. They didn't look all that different, other than wing size or white feathers as opposed to brown or speckled. "This one," I told my grandma, pointing to a chicken that pecked seeds from my hand. Its "pak" sounded like a purr. I stroked the feathers and its beak nudged my hand.

"Not that one, Katya." Her pet Russian name for me. In the Catskills, we were all called by our Russian names.

I pouted. "But I really like her."

My grandmother gave me a hug and walked over to the chicken man and whispered something. He shook his head no, and my grandma spoke quietly but firmly, waving her hands for punctuation. Finally, the man sighed and put my favorite chicken into a cage in the truck.

I plopped myself back on the bench and sulked. I saw my seven-year-old sister Julie (Yulya) sitting in our cottage, peeking through a window, and motioned for her to come outside. She shook her head no and closed the blinds. That's when Sasha sat down beside me.

"You sure you want to be watching this?" he asked.

"Why not?" I still thought there was going to be some special chicken ceremony, and even though I couldn't get my favorite chicken, I'd be fine with another one for a pet.

He shrugged. "My kid brother wants nothing to do with it."

"Neither does my sister." It bothered me that he called his brother a kid, since he was my age. "Maybe they just don't like chickens."

For some reason, this made him laugh. "Which one is yours?"

"Well, I wanted the one with the white feathers. It ate right out of my hand, but my grandma didn't let me have it. Now it's in the truck."

His eyes widened, like something clicked. "What do you think is going to happen?" His voice was soothing when he said this, like he was talking to a little kid. I wasn't a little kid.

I got huffy. "What do you mean? We're getting chickens!"

But even as the words came out, I began to realize that wasn't what was going to happen. I didn't know what was, but I was pretty sure I wouldn't get a pet.

The chicken man stepped into the pen and the chickens squawked loudly. He picked one up and the chickens went crazy, running around the pen, squawking a chorus of protests. Sasha gripped the top of my arm. "I don't think you should stay for this."

I jerked my arm free. "I can if you can."

"You don't get it. They're not just *giving* them away."

I bit my lip. My voice shook. "What do you mean?"

The man took out a knife.

"Just go," said Sasha.

But I wouldn't. I needed to see what would happen.

The man gripped the chicken above the neck and sliced straight across the throat with his butcher knife. I gasped as the blood flowed from the hole. Tears fell down my cheeks. Then, the chicken flapped its wings and flew a few feet in the air, no head and all, before flopping back down for good.

It's then that I felt Sasha's hand tightly on mine. "I'm sorry," he said as I cried into his shoulder

When we saw each other after that, we only said hi and kept on walking. He played with the boys, I played with the girls. The next time I was that close to him again, I was thirteen and his lips were centimeters from mine and something had changed in his eyes.

| Spring |

Julie

The only cherries you see in Cherry Hill are in the super-market. There are no hills blooming with them—no trees either. Back when it was first named Cherry Hill, the land was a farm. As far as I know, the farm did not grow cherries. My best friend Chloe says calling it Cherry Hill is ironic, but obviously words are not her strong suit. That's not what ironic means. No, the name Cherry Hill is a misnomer, and a sad one at that. Just ask my mom.

She and her parents moved to the United States from some small "backwards Russian hole" when she was in high school. They lived in Brighton Beach, New York, which made my grandparents ecstatic and annoyed the heck out of my mom. Living in Brighton Beach—where all stores were Russian-owned, where there was no need to learn English—was the same as being back in Russia, she said. She was bigger than that.

For college, my mom got a scholarship and went to

California. She loved the glitz and said it was her kind of place. Somewhere along the way, she met my dad. By that time, the Cali glamor was burning her out. Dad was from Cherry Hill, and she thought there would be fields and fields of colorful flowers and cherry trees under which she could rest and dream. This place, she thought, would be all beautiful, the kind of place she deserved.

When I was ten, I thought I'd fix things for her. Katie had just painted some dorky pic of a cherry tree, which mom loved. No, more than loved—adored, revered. It seemed to make her crazy happy. That Mother's Day, I got us matching headbands with saved birthday and lunch money. Since Mom liked it when she and Katie wore the same styles, I thought it was the perfect gift. The headbands were silver in color, with red plastic cherries intertwined at the top and little green stems as accents. Mom put hers on right away and smiled real big. I put mine on too and ran to get a mirror so we could see what we looked like in these identical bands. Mom put her arm around me, smile still on her face. "Julie, honey," she said, "I don't think this is quite right for you. I think you need to grow into it."

Grow into a headband? I thought. What the heck did *that* mean? "We'll get you one that works better with your coloring." A week later, she got me a new headband. It was brown and plain and not pretty at all. I put it on for her anyway, and she nodded. "Perfect. One day you'll grow into the other one. Until then, maybe Katie should wear it?"

Katie took it. She wore it all the time. The cherries bloomed on her head the way they never would on mine.

Even when Katie stopped wearing the cherries—"too babyish for high school"—Mom still kept it, and I caught her taking it out of her drawer to stare at them. She never gave the headband back to me. I'm thirteen now, and I guess I still haven't grown into it. But each time she takes it out, she mumbles about being tricked and manipulated and glares at my dad. He says he never described Cherry Hill the way Mom says he did. That it was my mom's own creation.

It really doesn't matter. Either way, she's stuck here—waiting for cherries that will never bloom.

Katie

H i, baby," says Ethan, sidling up against me at my locker. He grabs me and pulls me to him, and I drop my books and wrap my arms around his neck.

My cheerleading skirt swishes against his basketball shorts, and we're the perfect picture. East High's star point guard and newly crowned Pyramid Girl.

Someone shouts "Get a room!" and Ethan sticks up his middle finger at them, all the while his lips not leaving mine.

I don't know how long we're there, kissing amidst the chaos of the hallways, amidst the hoots and hollers and lewd, teasing remarks. Mr. Stevens, last year's biology teacher, clears his throat and gives a halfhearted "Move it along," but we ignore him and he moves along. When the bell rings to signal the start of homeroom, we ignore that too. Because teachers pretend not to notice when Ethan saunters in late. Because they fall for his basketball jersey and wide smile and slam dunks. Because I'm up on the list too. I'm Pyramid Girl.

And not just Pyramid Girl, but Pyramid Girl as a *sophomore*. Because the two of us together are power, are invincible.

When the next bell rings for first period, we ignore it too. Because we can.

Kyle

You watch your mother hop around in the kitchen, putting on a tasseled boot with one hand and applying lipstick with the other.

"What?" she says, jumping into the other boot. "Don't I look all right?"

You shrug. At sixteen, you're not an expert on women, or even girls, so what can you offer? "You look fine."

"Gee, thanks," she says, kissing you on the forehead and grabbing her purse. "You sure know how to make a lady feel good."

You shudder. She doesn't notice. Maybe you only shuddered on the inside.

"All right then. Numbers for take-out are on the fridge. I'll be home the usual." Same speech each time, and yet she feels the need to repeat herself.

"Got it. Have fun." That's your usual response, too.

"If only." Then she's gone to pay the bills, and you

11

choose not to think about how. If you do, if you allow yourself to think about the snide remarks your friends make, their description of your mom's body as she slides down the pole, then you won't be able to eat. Some days you purposely think about it so you can punish yourself or punish her, but today you're hungry.

You grab the menu for Casa de Fajitas and order the usual. You smile when you hang up the phone. The meal will be extra good because your older brother Alex hates Mexican. You could have compromised and ordered Italian or Chinese—foods the both of you like—but you're the one who always compromises. Always plays the yes man. Always acts so ... conciliatory, as your English teacher once put it, because you have never challenged her on a grade, not even when it was obvious she was wrong. Who needs the conflict? But being so agreeable tears at you. You wonder what would happen if you ever stood your ground. Argued. Said no. It's not like you've never tried, but you gave up too easily. Feared too much.

You're devouring one of your chicken fajitas when Alex and girl du jour walk into the kitchen. The GDJ reeks of peroxide and chemicals, a smell you recognize from the salon your mom used to work in. As a kid, the smell brought you comfort. Most of your mom's clients were older women and they brought you cookies and pinched your cheeks. They made you feel safe. But too many of Alex's hookups smell this way. It only chills you now.

Alex waves his hand in front of his face as if fanning away noxious odors. "You order ass again, bro?"

"Have some," you say, shoving the fajita under his nose, hoping his disgust for Mexican will send him out of the kitchen.

GDJ grabs the untouched fajita on your plate and takes a large bite. You cringe. Why does he always bring such gross girls home? Or maybe that's the point. They prove his effed-up theories true.

"Sure," you say. "Have some too."

"Sooorry," says GDJ, shaking her peroxide hair and spreading the fumes more. She doesn't sound sorry at all.

"Don't you worry," says Alex in his I'm-the-cool-big-brother voice. "She'll make it up to you." He leers at GDJ, and she winks like she actually knows what he's talking about. I wonder what he's going to do next year, after he's graduated and won't have an entire high school of girls to choose from.

I count down the days to when I'll be roaming those halls without worrying about his shadow or the remains of some girl he's screwed over.

GDJ whispers something in Alex's ear, and he laughs. "You better believe it, but leave the fajita stench here. I don't want it in my room."

"Later," says GDJ to you as she grabs Alex's hand. He squeezes her ass, and she squeals.

The click of stilettos gets quieter as they head to Alex's room. You don't smell Mexican anymore, only processed hair. You put your head in your hands and wait until Alex calls you. You could leave, but if it's not her, there would be someone else.

Alex

Today my mother is dressed like a freaking church lady. Dress that stops inches above her ankles, sleeves that go to her wrists, and a lacy collar.

"What gives, Mary?" I ask. "Confession time?"

"I don't have time for your bullshit today," she says, putting on her schoolmarm black pumps.

"Whoa, whoa. Harsh words for a religious woman."

"Jesus, Alex—" She drops her bag and Avon makeup spills all over the floor. "Goddamn," she mutters.

I shake my head. "And the Lord's name in vain, too."

She scrambles to pick up the makeup and I don't help her. Sometimes, I feel guilty acting like an ass to her, but today is not one of those rare days. I'm still curious about the getup, though. Normally when she's headed to one of her jobs, she looks like a whore. I pick up a lipstick and hand it to her. "So really. What's the deal?" Virgin Mary she's not.

She sighs. "I'm peddling makeup to a church choir. They're trying to attract a more modern audience. I'm giving them makeovers."

I whistle. "You never miss an opportunity."

She glares at me. "Can't you ever act human?" She points to the refrigerator and recites her take-out menu speech. I say a mental thank you to whoever/whatever that I'm home before Kyle today. Three days since he ordered Mexican and the place still smells like diarrhea.

"Later," I say. She drops a fifty on the table before heading to the door. "And don't worry. You look totally saintlike. Just hope none of them bring their husbands." She slams the door and I call for pizza. It's here in under twenty minutes.

"Hey baby," says Jasmine, my favorite pizza slut, when I open the door. "Haven't seen you in a while. What's up with that?"

"I haven't been in the mood for pizza."

"Oh yeah? Are you in the mood now?" She comes in before I have a chance to invite her and kicks the door shut with her foot. I take the pizza from her and walk toward the kitchen, knowing she will follow. They always do.

I open the box, take out a slice, and tease her with it before putting it in my mouth. She crosses her arms across her tits, creating cleavage. Not sure if she's doing that on purpose. I take my time chewing the slice, and she flips, just like I knew she would. "Seriously?" she says. "I don't have all effing night."

I chew slower. I don't know why she thinks the rules are any different tonight. Like I'd ever let her be in charge. That's not how it works.

She clenches her fists. "Fine, asshole. I don't need this shit. I'm outta here." If I didn't know better, I'd have believed her. She's a pretty good actress, better than most. That's actually what she's saving her pizza money for—more acting lessons and commuting money for auditions.

I give her the fifty. "Got change?"

She curses and fumbles in her apron for some bills, then throws them on the table and storms to the door. I wonder if she really thinks she'll get me to grovel. I wait until I hear her turn the knob and call out, "Jasmine?"

"Yeah?" The smile in her voice makes me laugh. She thinks I'm going to ask her to come back.

"Don't forget to turn the lock before you go. I'd get up myself but I'm really liking your pie."

"Fuck you!" she calls, but I hear her turn the lock before slamming the door shut.

Katie

My mother is in the bleachers today for the playoffs, wearing our school colors—blue and gold. She even put blue and gold streamers in her hair like the cheerleaders did. "Those were my best days," she always says to me. When I became Pyramid Girl two months ago, she cried. Hugged me so tight and wanted me to show her my winning routine (even though she'd seen me practice it dozens of times). She called her friends with the "big news." We squealed together and went out for blueberry ice cream with yellow sprinkles. "You made it, Katie," she said. When Ethan asked me out days later, we screamed again, jumping up and down in the kitchen. "Can you *believe* your big sister?" she asked Julie.

Julie rolled her eyes. "Oh, I believe it. I'm screaming on the inside. Can't you hear me?"

Mama dragged Julie to today's game, and while Mama is all smiles and eager, Julie is playing games on her cell. Maybe when she's in high school next year, she'll see it differently. How awesome, how amazing it all is.

The band starts their drumroll and Mama's streamers

bounce. The announcer's voice booms out. "AND NOW, LET'S MEET OUR EAST HIGH CRUSADERS!"

We cheerleaders assemble in front of the boys' locker room door. We shake our pom-poms and do high kicks before forming a tunnel for the basketball players to run through. We each have a number that we scream extra loud, kick extra high, jump extra big for. Mine is "NUMBER 23, POINT GUARD, ETHAN SCHMIDT!" The crowd yells "Schmiiiddy" and stomps their feet on the bleachers. I throw my pom-poms in the air and do a back handspring, then a split as Ethan makes his way through the tunnel. He lifts me high in the air and kisses me until I can't breathe and runs to the center of the court.

The crowd is on their feet, cheering. "Give him some more good luck, Katie!" someone shouts. I cartwheel to him and press my lips on his again, and the other cheerleaders surround us, shaking their pom-poms.

More players are called to the court and the crowd and cheerleaders scream louder. I wave my pom-poms extra high for Ethan's best friend—"NUMBER 54, CENTER, CHRIS MAIN!" The crowd explodes—"Yeah, Maniac!"— and Marissa, the one who was next in line for Pyramid Girl, does a forward handspring and a split in the air. She smirks at me like I should worry, but I don't. The smirk is all she'll do, because I know about her and Mr. Stevens. She told me about their kisses, back when we were friends. Back when we practiced our routines together. Before I soared to the top of the pyramid and she became second-best.

But I'll never tell. If our roles were reversed, she would,

so she just throws looks my way and hopes I'm not vengeful like her.

Next up is Julie's math tutor, "NUMBER 12, GUARD DEREK SANTOS!" "Yeah, Sandog!" the crowd bellows. Our co-captains, Trina and Leah, boost me in the air and I flip coming down. Marissa fumes.

Soon, the rest of the team is on the court and a chorus soloist is getting ready to sing "The Star Spangled Banner." The gym is silent. Our heads our bowed, our hands on our hearts. And then we're on "the home of the brave" and the noise erupts again. I get ready for our hello cheer, making sure the glitter is in my pockets. Ethan runs up to me one last time. He drags me to the center of the court, lifts me up on his shoulders, and holds the basketball high. "This game is for my baby!" he yells. I laugh, and the crowd laughs, and he kisses me one last time before heading back to his position.

It's crazy, and it's wild, and my mother is beaming on the bleachers, and I think hands lift me up to the top of the pyramid.

But maybe I just fly up there.

Julie

I am not a basketball girl. I'm a nose-in-book, Word Masters, Math Olympiad kind of chick. And sitting here, watching big sister dazzle with extra-wide splits, is torture.

Something else that's torture: my mother watching Katie like those pom-poms have hypnotizing powers. Her blue and gold ribbons match Katie's (don't even get me started on that weirdness). She made me wear my blue sweater, and I did because I thought that maybe we could bond over the silliness of it. No, I'm lying. She would never think it silly. I just hoped we could bond.

Only in basketball could my sister suck face like the guy is her oxygen mask and the crowd applaud her for it. Mama is looking at me like I should be proud, like *I* should want that. I don't. Until Derek Santos runs onto the court.

Derek is perfection. He's a jock, but he knows his numbers. The boy can add digits in his head like he has a calculator in there. He's tutoring me for the Math Olympiad. Kudos to Katie for making that happen. He waves at me from the court, and for a few seconds, basketball is interesting. Katie shows off with a special cheer and then turns to me and points, like she's saying she's doing it for me. I smile and nod like I get it. Heck, she's trying, and it's not her fault Mama loves her best. Or that every boy swoons at her feet.

Derek, at least, doesn't look like he's swooning. He waved at me. *At me.* With the hand that a few days ago squeezed my knee.

The cheerleaders begin their "Hello" cheer. Katie is lifted above everyone's shoulders. She's beaming like she's reached the heavens. Like she could touch the sky for real. She puts her arms up in a V and claps in rhythm. She throws her pom-poms in the air and the girl below her catches them. The crowd cheers. My mother dabs at her eyes. "Victory!" the cheerleaders shout, their tops shimmering.

Then they lift Katie higher. She reaches into her pockets, and the girls throw her toward the ceiling. Gold glitter flies through the air—on Katie, on the rest of the team. The overhead fans blow it into the bleachers. It's raining gold, and Mama jumps up to catch as many sparkles as she can. I clench my fists and close my eyes against the rain.

But then it stops. I open my fists and they're filled with gold.

Kyle

Alex texts you in study hall: Treats tonight.

That can only mean one thing, and your stomach clenches.

Who is it this time? Someone new? Someone used? You prefer new because that means you'd be expected to do less, not continue from wherever you left off the last time.

You could choose to not come home. Tonight. Maybe ever. But that's a nice fantasy. Where would you go?

"Hey, kid." And it's him, right beside you. Looking normal in jeans and a sweatshirt, like so many other guys in your school. "Get my text?"

You nod.

"What's with the face? You look like you're gonna yak."

You are. You start to get up but the library spins. You sit again.

"Shit, why don't you go to the nurse or something? I don't need to be catching your disease."

You would, but you can't get up.

You take deep breaths. "I'll be fine," you say.

"Hope so," says Alex, slapping you on the back. "Can't have you missing out on the fun. This one is eager and willing." He cracks his knuckles and laughs. "Kind of like that one." He points to Sarah, and that makes you sicker. How did you not notice her?

You want to punch him. Watch his head explode and the contents scatter all over the room. He's sneering at you now, daring you, knowing you're too weak to fight him, too weak to even say no.

But at least you can leave at this moment. You shake off the nausea, the red haze of anger, the spinning room. You get to your feet and walk out. You leave him.

For now.

Katie

Big night for you tonight," says Ethan, assuming his position beside me in the hallway.

"For us," I say, and he puts his arm around my waist and we head to the caf.

As we walk through the halls, I feel the eyes. The thoughts swirling around us of people wishing they could be us. "Party!" someone shouts. We lost the playoff game, but it doesn't matter. There's the party.

So many smiles and hugs. "Smooches!" shouts Leah as she passes us in the hall. "Coronation night, girl!"

I laugh like she's being silly, like it's no big deal. But Pyramid Girl is *everything*—even the teachers congratulated me when I got the position. And this party is everything, since it sets the stage for football cheerleading next year. It's all I've thought about—with every jump, every roll, every split—for months. As if without it, the top of the pyramid wouldn't really be mine.

"Dude," yells Chris, sidling up beside us. He slaps Ethan

on the back. Ethan play-fights him back. "Mrs. Schmidt," he says, nodding solemnly.

I giggle. Ethan leans in close to me, his mouth by my ear. "I like the sound of that. We should consummate our marriage, don't you think?"

"I think I like the mystery," I tease, and he slaps my butt like we have an in-joke. But I don't want to consummate anything. He's asked me, but all we've done is a lot of kissing. And I'd like to keep it that way for a while.

When we get to our lunch table, it erupts in applause and hands banging on the table and feet stomping on the floor. "Kaaatie! Pyramid Girl!" they shout. "Schmiiiddy!" This has been our greeting, day after day, for two months. It's a routine that can never get old, that still makes my heart thump with excitement.

Ethan bows, and I curtsy, and milk shoots out of Chris's nose. And the table laughs more. The teachers give us looks—crosses between reprimand and wistfulness.

"Huddle," shouts Ethan, and we do it.

I'm lifted high into the air to cheer for today's lunch: pizza.

Everyone's watching, dying, applauding, laughing. Everyone but Marissa. She just stares up at me, her smile toothy, her eyes cold and jealous. She's a junior. She should have been next, but I was lighter and my cartwheels were bigger and my jumps higher. When the list came out, she sputtered and shoved me aside.

"Let's hear it for pizza!" Ethan shouts.

Some kids at the lunch tables roll their eyes, but they watch us anyway.

"Give me a P!" Trina shouts.

"P!" I pump my arm in the arm.

"Give me an I!" yells Chris.

"Maaainiac!" someone hollers.

"I!" I pump my other arm. Leah tosses me a bunch of crumpled up napkins to use as pom-poms.

"Z, Z, A!" others hoot.

"What's that spell?" asks Leah.

"Pizza, pizza, pizza today!" I yell, throwing my napkins into the air before falling into Ethan's arms.

Even the teacher on lunch duty is laughing. The bell rings and we gather our things, leaving uneaten pizza on our plates, crumpled-up napkins on the floor. I move to pick them up but Ethan pulls me along. He says something to Chris and they both laugh before Chris walks away.

"You're awesome," says Ethan, pulling me in for a kiss.

I laugh. "You're awesomer."

The cafeteria doors part, like the Red Sea, and we're out.

Julie

I'm just glad Katie and I are not in the same school yet. The way she prances at home, the way her cell goes off every three seconds to "Popular" (I'm not lying), the way Mama makes her favorite foods *every night*. It's good to have a break for a few hours, a place where no one knows or cares who Katie is.

"You get too worked up about her," Chloe says now, chowing down on her burger and fries at McD's. "What's the big?"

I take two fries from her and savor them before dipping my apple "fries" into the caramel sauce (Mama would know if I had a whole serving of fries). "It's just, like, she has everything. No one person should have everything."

Chloe laughs. "Puh-leeze. You're such a drama queen. No one has everything."

I hate when Chloe puts on her mature act. "Well," I say huffily, "to my mother, Pyramid Girl is everything. She was Pyramid Girl once too."

Chloe rolls her eyes. "Whatever. Let's talk about

something else. How's the math tutoring going?" She elbows me and winks.

"Derek Santos put his hand on my knee. Again." I whisper it. Who knows who could be listening?

Chloe raises her eyebrows. "Like how?"

We dissect it and I show her and we both agree that the positioning and the way he did it seems more than just friendly tutor/student.

By the time I get home, I'm feeling better. I'm imagining what spot on me Derek will touch next. I'm thinking that if someone sees me—just me, not the me standing beside Katie—I may actually look cute. I'm even proud of myself for sticking to the apple slices.

Then I walk into my kitchen and it's a Katie fashion show.

"Oh Julie!" says my mother. "Thank goodness you're home. We could really use your help pinning up Katie's hair."

Katie looks almost apologetic, but she doesn't say she doesn't need me. I sigh. And play. "So, tell me about this night of yours."

Katie shrugs. "It's just a party. Like a welcome-to-the-top-of-the-pyramid thing." She plays it down, for my sake I guess, but I can see her wanting to bounce, see her toes wiggling with excitement in their sparkly pumps. Her eyes shine in the same way mine did when I got the highest Word Masters score in the school. No one threw me a party for that. No one pinned *my* hair up when I got my ribbon.

My mother moves a strand of hair from Katie's eyes and steps back to get a better look. Her eyes shine with pride.

"Ethan won't be able to take his eyes off of you," she says, and Katie beams.

"And what about Alex?" I ask.

Katie's smile wavers. We don't talk about Alex during the school year. Part of their idiotic arrangement. But they hook up every summer. How does she NOT think about him? I mean, Philly is only twenty minutes away.

"He's my summer boyfriend," she says, like it's that easy.

"And if Ethan wants to date in the summer?" Nothing should be this easy.

"Oh, Julie!" Katie ruffles my hair like I'm ten instead of thirteen. "I know what I'm doing."

Mama fixes a bobby pin on Katie's head that I already put in. "Today is your sister's big night. No need to make trouble, okay?"

I close my mouth and fix Katie's hair. By the time she leaves the house, she's perfection, and my fingers smell like hair spray.

I wish I'd eaten more fries with Chloe.

Alex

"Yo!" I yell when I walk into the townhouse. "Asswipe, you home?"

No one answers, and Jasmine giggles. I hate when she does that. It sounds so fake and innocent, and Jasmine is far from innocent.

"Looks like the coast is clear," she says.

She moves to pull me toward my bedroom, then stops. That's right. I'm the leader. But I know what she wants, and I'm not going to be a dick.

"I missed you," I say into her neck, and carry her to my bedroom.

She nuzzles her head against my neck with a small moan, and I put her down on the bed and get on top of her.

"Tell me you only want me," she whispers.

I want to laugh, but I can't risk her walking out on my hard-on. "I only want you." *Because you're the one who's here.*

She pulls my shirt over my head, and I rip a button taking off hers. She moans extra loud like she's a fucking porn star. And she wonders why I won't commit. I don't commit to whores.

But they keep me going until I see Katya. She's too good for this kind of shit.

I pull off my jeans and move her mouth to where so many have gone before, and let her show her talents. Gotta hand it to her, she knows what she's doing.

When I'm done, she moves my hand to her underwear, and I hear the front door open.

"Hold that thought," I say.

Then I cover her with a blanket—the little shit scares so easy, I always have to ease him in—and run to get Kyle.

Katie

Chris's house is decorated with blue and gold streamers, and the party is in full swing when Ethan and I get there.

"It's Ethan and Katie!" yell Leah and Trina when I walk through the double doors into the foyer. Drunk partiers throw confetti on me and Ethan.

"Schmiiidy!"

"Pyramid Girl!"

They give us blue drinks, served in blue plastic cups. Ethan clinks his cup with mine. "To us," he says, staring deeply into my eyes. I get the meaning behind the stare and look away.

"To us," I say. The sweet liquid tastes like a blue Jolly Rancher and goes down easy. Everyone cheers as we chug it.

"Bro!" yells Chris, putting one arm around my shoulder, the other around Ethan's. I'm wearing a gold halter top and his hand feels cold on my shoulders. I shrug it away. He seems to give Ethan a look.

"Can I borrow your man for a few minutes?" he asks. "Guy stuff."

Trina is right beside me. "Take him. We have our own things to talk about it."

"Don't forget to miss me," says Ethan, kissing me hard, running his hands under my top. Someone whoops and whistles.

"Boys are so needy," Trina says when they leave. "Who cares, though, right? We have to make your crown!"

There's *really* going to be a crown? She drags me to an upstairs bedroom, where the other cheerleaders are crafting. They're holding a gold plastic crown and gluing fake jewels to it. I finger the materials they're putting on. Smooth rubies, blue velvet for the trim, diamonds, sapphires. I know they're probably from the dollar store, but they sparkle like they're real.

"Try it on," says Leah, when it dries.

I do, and they *ooh*. I run to the mirror. It's perfect and shiny and matches my top.

"You look hot," says Trina.

"Totally hot," says everyone else. Even Marissa nods, but she looks pretty drunk. "Shots!" she yells, and Leah pulls a bottle of bubblegum vodka from under the bed.

I've never done shots, but they're poured and everyone is chanting. I down my quickly, and it's fizzy and tastes like pink bubble gum with a burn. "Again!" Trina shouts, and we all do another. And then one more.

"Save some for the king!" The door bangs open and

there's Ethan, crown on his head. But it's flimsier than mine. I think it's from Burger King.

He scoops me up and someone says "Aww," like there's nothing more romantic than our crowns beside each other.

"Let's get this party back downstairs," Leah says, pushing everyone out, but she's getting wasted too and keeps tripping.

"You heard the lady," says Chris. "Besides, I have a better idea!"

And everyone runs downstairs, laughing, shouting, screaming. My pump snags on the carpet but Ethan is there to catch me. "My Romeo," I say, and he pushes me to the floor. I can tell I'm getting tipsy because the floor feels like it's moving. I can feel his hand on the zipper of my jeans, but by the time I react, the zipper is down.

He gets off me, shrugging. "Sorry about that. You're just so hot, I can't help it."

I open my mouth to say something, but my brain is mushy. Then Chris is pulling us down the stairs, telling us this amazing idea he has of me and Ethan doing a keg stand in unison.

"King and queen together! It will be epic!"

And everyone is agreeing with him. "Totally epic!"

And Leah and Trina get the cheerleaders going in a cheer, betting that I can beat Ethan. And in my drunken haze I think I *can*. I'm Pyramid Girl!

They take off our crowns before the world goes upside down, and I drink and don't stop until I choke. They get me down and put my crown back on, but Ethan is still going.

They bring him down next and raise his arm high in the air. "The winner!"

"I guess I beat you," says Ethan, crown looking higher than before. "The king rules. Don't forget it!"

"The king rules!" the room shouts.

Then he leans in close, his arms holding me up. "Are you okay? Do you want to lie down? You'll be all right."

"Thanks," I slur, and I think what a great guy he is. How lucky I am that he wants to take care of me.

I let him lead me to a room, let him lay me down on the bed. Chris's beagle is on it, and he stirs. Ethan moves the dog to the corner of the bed. His words are soothing. He strokes my hair. He leaves and then is back with water. "Drink," he says, and I do.

The room is still spinning, but I don't feel sick. Just high and happy and dizzy. And tired.

He lays down beside me and strokes my stomach. I turn to him and kiss him, and I love that our crowns are still on.

I let his hands roam under my shirt. I like that he tells me I'm beautiful. I could just lie on this bed and only kiss for hours. But I'm getting so tired. I feel my eyes closing. I feel him kissing me and I'm in and out. Something wet on my toes. The beagle is licking them. Ethan's hands move to my jeans, and I move mine to push him away. At least I think I do. I want to, but the room spins faster. The jeans are off, and he's pulling at my underwear, and I whisper, "No."

And he says, "It will be okay. I promise. You're my Pyramid Girl."

And I want to ask him *why rush*, and tell him not

tonight, but the words don't come and my eyes keep closing. And he's still telling me—voice sounding further away than before—that it will be okay and in my haze I believe him. I'm Pyramid Girl.

Then there's pain. My eyes snap open, and Ethan is rocking on top of me. I want to push him off, but I can't. I close my eyes, hoping to erase the pain, to disappear. He stops. I breathe. But then he's on top of me again, rougher than before, hurting me more. I open my eyes again, and it's not Ethan anymore. He's beside me now, still telling me it will be okay, still calling me his Pyramid Girl, telling me to relax, to sshh…

As Chris pushes further inside me.

Katie

The morning after, I wake up on the floor, naked, musty blanket over me. Beagle licking my toes again. The room still spins, and I grab the blanket and run to the bathroom to throw up. So many colors in the porcelain. I let go of the blanket and hold the sides of the toilet. More keeps coming. I pull the blanket over me again and slump down on the floor and wait for the next wave.

Footsteps enter and feet stand beside me. "You mind?" asks Chris, pulling down his pants and peeing into the bowl.

Funny that he asks me now. He didn't ask last night. Peeing must be more intimate than sex to him.

My head pounds. I feel it splitting. I shiver and push him out of the way so I can throw up again.

"Jeez, now you made me get some on the floor." He grabs toilet paper and wipes up his pee as I continue to throw up. "I'll get you some water."

When he comes back, I'm empty. I take the glass and he hangs around, staring at the blanket. I pull it tighter around me. "You can go."

He smiles. "You know…" He walks closer, bends down, puts his hand under the blanket, touches me. "I'd say we should have another go, if you didn't look so wrecked."

"Go to hell."

"That's not what you said last night." He winks at me.

I couldn't have said I wanted to, could I? The night is a blur. I remember the dog. Ethan on top of me, then not Ethan. Eyes closing and opening. "Where's Ethan?"

Chris laughs. "Yeah, he had to jet. You don't think you're still together, do you? Another guy might have been able to hack it, but not Ethan. You can't sleep with a guy's best friend and expect him to still want to be with you. There's a code, girl."

"I didn't—"

Chris nods. "No, I get it. You were trashed. I told him that. Told him to give you another chance." He shrugs. "What can you do?"

My mouth is dry. I stare at him and wonder if he's real. Maybe I died from alcohol poisoning and I'm in hell. Maybe that's where I was last night. Maybe none of it happened.

He comes close, wipes at the tear down my cheek. "Hey now. It's okay. Who cares about Ethan? You can have me anytime you want me. I'm not as stuck up as Ethan. Shit, you're almost a virgin."

Oh God. Oh God. Oh God. This *has* to be hell.

"Wait," he says, running into the bedroom. "I know what will cheer you up."

He comes back with my crown. How is it intact? Still shiny. Still fake.

"Look, I don't mean to be a dick, but my parents will be home in an hour. Drink some more water, get dressed, and then I have to get you home. Okay?"

I nod and dry heave into the toilet.

"And, don't worry about me saying anything. I know girls are weird like that. I doubt Ethan will say anything either."

I stare at the stupid crown.

"Chin up, babe. Don't forget who you are. You're Pyramid Girl!"

Julie

For more than a month now, Katie has been moping around the house playing reverse dress-up. Each morning, it's a different combination of sweatpants and T-shirt. The only days I see her make any kind of effort is when she has cheer practice. Then it's cheerleading skirt, ribbons, and cheer shirt like the rest of the sheep.

Mama speaks softly to her, like she will break any minute. She plots ways to get Ethan back. Ignores Katie when she says he likes someone else now, they just grew apart. It's just high school, Mama.

Chloe says to expect more days like this. When her older sister, who's in college, got dumped by her boyfriend, it was waterworks every day. Katie doesn't cry, though, just walks around like a zombie. She put a big calendar on her wall and crosses out the days until the lake house in red ink.

One step closer to Sasha. One step closer to Katya.

Today, Derek is coming over to help me study again. Maybe that will cheer her up. She always got along with him. Normally, I hate when boys come here because they forget I ever existed. But Derek already knows Katie, and he chose *me*. Three weeks ago, he was quizzing me on sample problems in my room. He played it cool, pretending to trip and pulling me down on the bed with him. His lips weren't clumsy at all, so that's how I know he planned it.

But then I made one mistake. His kiss must have injected me with a dose of crazy, because that's the only way I can explain telling Mama about it. She was making dinner, cracking eggs into a pan. I gave her all the details, like she was Chloe or something. "He must think I'm pretty," I said, smiling.

She took a break from her pan and tapped her fingernails on the table. For a second, I thought she would hug me. She had *that* look, but instead she patted my hand. "If you think so," she said. "Help me with dinner?"

But she'll see when he comes today. She'll see I'm not crazy and imagining things. She'll see boys like me, just like they do Katie.

Katie

Ethan has been giving me funny looks all day. So has Marissa. Did he tell her about the party? I pretend I don't notice the two of them staring at me. Trina and Leah stop me at my locker after school and tell me I need an intervention.

"You need to stop moping about Ethan," says Leah, like this is an ordinary breakup.

"Besides," says Trina, her voice low like she's letting me in on some juicy gossip, "I hear someone else likes you." This last part she sings, like I should be jumping up and down, excited that some other boy in this hole wants to date me.

"I'll give you a hint," says Leah. "He's on the team, too, and just as hot, and it will make Ethan crazy jealous."

I get chills. I don't care who it is. I don't want anyone. I want to go to the lake house and start over and see Alex and be Katya.

But they're looking at me, waiting for me to jump. "Who?" I ask, plastic cheerleader smile on.

"Chris," they say in unison. "Can you just die?"

I thought I already did.

Julie

It's two weeks before summer vacation, and Chloe is planning a pool party for after the eighth grade graduation ceremony.

When I tell Mom, her eyes bug out.

"But why? You can't tell me she actually *wants* to wear a bathing suit." She's nibbling on a carrot stick, which means she's on another diet. If she keeps eating it that slowly she'll make it last through tomorrow, which is probably her intent.

I shrug. "Why *not*?" I don't look at her when I say this because I know exactly why not. I know how my mom's world works, how the real world—as she sees—it works. Girls named Chloe are supposed to be blond-haired and twiggy. *My* Chloe has brown hair that fills up with split ends too quickly. She wears mismatched pants and shirts and carries a pocketbook that's three sizes bigger than what's in style. She's pudgy, and when she swims, she wears huge goggles over her glasses. Mom once said that her parents should never have named her Chloe, like someone should have looked past the baby covered in placenta drippings and figured out that the name wouldn't suit her as a teen.

"Oh please, Julie." She waves her hand dismissively. "Don't act all dumb and innocent. It's not becoming on you."

Here we go.

"Honestly, I feel sorry for Chloe." Mom takes another nibble of carrot. "What kind of mother lets her daughter prance around looking like … like … *that*? You, for instance, will *not* be wearing any skimpy bathing suits. We'll get you one of those fancy kinds that pull everything in and a little skirt to mask everything else." Large bite of carrot and it's gone. She frowns and opens a new bag.

Here's the thing. My plan is to go to the party and sit on a recliner and eat chips and pizza. The thought of putting on *any* kind of bathing suit, thinning or not, is not on my agenda. And honestly, I think it's cool that Chloe never cares about what anyone else thinks. People come to her parties. Sure, not the most popular crowd, but a good bunch and it's always fun.

I open my mouth to tell my mother all of this and more. To tell her I don't care about what people think, either. To tell her I don't care what *she* thinks. But something else comes out instead.

"Sure," I say, grabbing one of her carrots. "That would be perfect. Maybe a black one." I nibble on the carrot and my mom smiles.

I smile back because I know the real truth. I'm not Chloe. I care too much.

Katie

Three days until the lake house and it's all I care about. My suitcase is packed and I keep closing my eyes, hoping to fall asleep and wake up when it's time to leave.

"Katie," says my mother, stopping at the doorway of my room. "What are you doing? Julie is at a pool party. Why aren't you out painting the town?"

I close my eyes again and rub my temples, hoping she'll disappear. I don't want parties where my mouth hurts from fake smiles and laughs. Where I can run into reminders of the past. "Home Depot ran out of colors I like."

Mom frowns. "What's that supposed to mean?" Then she smiles in her inviting way. I can almost see the signals from her brain to her mouth, telling it to be kind. She sits on my bed and strokes my hair. "Something happen you want to talk about? Were the other girls jealous? It's a way of life, I'm afraid."

Away away away. Her, me, I don't care. Just so long as I don't have to listen.

I turn away from her, but she keeps talking. "I

understand," she whispers. "Looking like we do has its price. But it's who we are."

It's all we are. That's what she'd like to say. *Capitalize on your looks.* I wonder sometimes if that *is* all that people will ever see when they look at me. On those days, I hold on tightest to that spot on the pyramid, the spot that people still think belongs to me. Like I'm same girl I was. On those days, cheerleading practice is all me. I cheer extra loud, smile extra wide, jump extra high. When the glitter falls, I pocket the stray pieces that cascade off my hair instead of letting them fall to the ground.

Those days, I want to text Alex and ask him to talk to me like a normal person. Like someone who knows a different Katie than everyone here knows. Not even a Katie. *Katya.*

But we don't talk during the year. There's something appealing about having our separate worlds and lives, me knowing nothing of his Philadelphia world, he not knowing the Katie who now lives in darkness while pretending to be in the light.

My mother grows silent and leaves, I think for good, but she's back minutes later, frame in hand.

I know what it is without her telling me, but she does anyway. "This is the tree you drew for me," she says. "This," she says again, holding the painting tightly, like it could fly away and take with it any remnants of her dreams, "shows me we're the same. We think alike. You need beauty, too."

I look at the picture in her hand and carefully trace the lines. The tree was supposed to echo Vincent van Gogh's painting of a cherry tree. My seventh grade art teacher spoke about the strokes van Gogh used, the quality of brush, the way the tree cascades to the grass. She wanted us to draw our own version of that painting. I took away the starkness I saw in van Gogh's painting, covered the naked, lonely branches. I painted leaves that appeared to rise out of the tree. They spread out, like they wanted nothing to do with the bark and instead clung to the branches. The pink mixed with the brown and green so it wasn't obvious where one color ended and another began. I added cherries, too. They clung to the branches, to the leaves; some found one another and huddled on the ground. My teacher didn't care that it didn't resemble van Gogh's style. She used it in an exhibition, talked about its beauty. But my mother loved it more.

She'd looked at it, speechless. "This," she'd said, "is where we were supposed to live." She may have said these words aloud, but they weren't meant for me. She hugged me tight. "Stay beautiful like this picture," she said. Then she ran out to have the painting matted.

Now I touch the frame again. Maybe she's right. Why else would I stray so much from the assignment? I feel her eyes on my face, see her head nod.

"I know you," she says.

No. You don't.

Today I used my art skills to cover permanent marker in a bathroom stall. I hadn't seen it before. I wonder if Ethan told someone, or maybe someone thought I needed a distraction from thinking about him, from moping about being dumped when I had everything they wanted. *For help with splits, call Katie Taylor. She knows how to spread 'em.*

I stared at it for a long time, trying to figure out if it was really there. Like I'd stared at Chris the morning after. Then I took out my pen and crayons from my art class and began to draw.

Branch after branch of ink and crayon to block out the words. I made the branches dark and thick and high, high, high. The words fell under their weight but did not go away.

I give the painting back to Mama. I don't tell her about the kinds of trees I draw now.

Instead, I smile. "A pool party is just what I need." Anything to get away.

I grab a red bikini out of my suitcase and go to the bathroom to get dressed. I leave Mom on my bed holding the painting close to her chest, imagining the perfect life for both of us within those trees.

Kyle

You watch the trees draw shadows on the shades, and it calms you. Your mother is out—as usual. Alex is out and will be for the entire night—not so usual. You were invited out, too. You were promised Girls. Beer. Beer-Goggled Girls. A celebration before "Junior Year Hell." For once, you thought about the invite. You don't usually do that. But then your bud Steve kept talking about the girls. How many he'd grab. How many he'd lay. How many beers he'd have to feed them so they'd be more willing to screw, but he wouldn't cross into the "is this date rape" gray. Your other friends egged him on, their mouths full of greasy pizza. They laughed and chocolate milk sprayed out their noses. This made you laugh, too. Hard. Like you haven't in a long time. "Shit," said Steve. "Looks like Kyle might actually come to something."

You punched him lightly in the arm. "Maybe."

The other guys laughed and snorted more, talked about how they'd divvy up the girls. Who they'd leave for you, who they'd share. And it was all in fun, but you got chills. You got hot. You felt the pizza making its way up to your mouth.

You swallowed it down. Took deep breaths while pretending to laugh. They mentioned *her*. Sarah. The laughter stopped. "Idiot," said Steve to the offender. "Sorry dude."

You laughed it off. You didn't like hearing her name. Didn't even let yourself think about her. Your friends thought they got it. They'd all been there, they said. One day you're carrying your girl's lunch tray. The next, you're not even on speaking terms. But it wasn't the same. You weren't like them. They didn't have a brother like yours, who ruined everything. Who you could never escape.

The bell rang for next period, took her out of your head, and the world moved again. Your friends slapped you on the back. "See you tonight, right?" said Steve. And you faked an enthusiastic, "Yeah, sure. You know it." But you knew you weren't going to any party. And that made you hate Alex more.

But now as you walk through the house, you feel at ease. The stench of Alex's cologne and faint cigarette smell still lingers, but he's not there. You breathe deeply and enjoy it. You order Mexican for dinner and eat both burritos in one sitting. The cheesy nachos, too. You lie on your bed and start on your summer reading list. You take a long shower. You call your grandparents to tell them you can't wait to see them at the lake house. "Oh, Kostya," they say, calling you your Russian name, and you smile because you like how time stops there. How all the grandparents still act like they're in the old country. How Katie's and Julie's grandpa—*dedushka*—picks berries and how their grandma—*babushka*—makes jam, saving a canister for your grandma. You like how the grandparents never learned much English and you're forced to remember Russian words you've forgotten during the year. Words your father used to say, that your mother never understood. You like that these are your dad's parents, and that you have them even though you'll never see your dad again. You like that you spend the summer in a small, two-bedroom cottage where it's too easy to see what everyone is doing. And you like that for the entire summer, you don't have to watch your back or think about what's next. For the whole summer, you can really breathe.

Alex

I'd rather breathe exhaust fumes than Catskills air, but I go for Katya. I load up the car and wait for Kyle to get his ass downstairs. "Let's go, loser," I holler, and my mom shakes her head.

"Can't you ever cut him any slack?" she says, but I know she wants us out of her hair. A whole summer without the kiddies. A whole summer to bring home any dick she wants.

"Aw, look who's decided to play mommy," I say. That went a little far. She takes a step toward me and raises her hand, then quickly puts it down. Yeah, I thought so. I'm wearing short sleeves today, and cross my arms so that she can see the scars from her assholes past. They're pretty faint, but not when you know where to look. She knows, but she doesn't.

"Kyle, let's go," she says. Her voice is tired. That's what hours on the pole does.

He finally bounds down the stairs, backpack slung over his shoulder. "Couldn't leave those SAT words behind for a minute, could you?" I say.

"Shut up, asshole."

"Did baby brother finally grow a pair?"

This time he ignores me. "See you soon, Mom," he says and gives her a stiff hug good-bye.

She holds him tight when he tries to pull away, and I swear she tears up. Geez, woman, don't you have to be around your kids to miss them when they go?

"Later, Mom," I say. I make no move to hug her, and she hangs back, too.

"Drive safe." She closes the door but continues to look through the window.

I peel out of the driveway and laugh when the tires screech. Kyle pastes himself to the door and closes his eyes.

"What the fuck is up with *you*?"

"Nothing," Kyle mumbles and keeps his eyes closed.

"Look, dickwad. It sucks enough that I have to go to this backwards shithole. I don't need you acting like a pansy the whole way there." I merge onto the highway and honk at an idiot trying to get into my lane.

Kyle's eyes snap open. "Why do you always have to be such an asshole?"

"Watch yourself," I say, and punch him hard in his arm. He winces. I want to tell Kyle he's lucky to have me to toughen him up. To look out for him. Something I never had. But he wouldn't get it.

"Why do you hate going to the lake house anyway? All you do is make out with Katie. That can't suck."

The phone vibrates in my pocket, and I wonder if that's her texting. Writing steamy things the two of us can do. A few days ago, she broke her own rule of not contacting me before summer. I guess she figured it was close enough. And thank God for that, because I was going crazy seeing the same chicks day in and day out. Playing their slutty games. Passing the time until I'd see Katya. These girls in Philly could learn from her. She wouldn't pull their shit, spreading her legs for just anyone. Not like I say no to that—I mean, it's free pussy. But sometimes it would be good to go where not every prick has been before, know what I mean?

"No, bro. Doesn't suck," I say, and smile. "She does, though."

"Maybe she practices, so she can be extra good."

I move to hit him but a car swerves in front of me and we avoid a massive collision. I turn my eyes back to the road and Kyle lets out a breath. Lucky break. He takes a book out of his backpack and starts reading, and I peek at my phone: MISS YOU <3.

Sweet and simple.

So why do I hate going there? Maybe because it's boring as all hell. Maybe because I hate when people are stuck in some past century. Maybe because I have to speak Russian because no one bothered to learn English. It's like my dad is laughing from heaven (hell?), telling me I can never let him go. The words are a reminder. My grandparents—his parents—are a reminder. The only one who seems to have moved on is my mother. Moved on way before he croaked. I hate that. How did she get to be so lucky?

Someone honks behind me and I realize I've slowed down below the speed limit. I've become *that* asshole. My phone vibrates again, and I gun the gas.

Katie

Dad spends the drive making small talk
He wants me to play trivia games
I'd rather text Sasha, remind him what he's
    been missing
Julie plays
Face contorted in thought
Glances at Mom for a reaction
But Mom is fixating on me
Eyes trying/prying to see my text
As usual
Caring too much

We hit traffic
Mom falls asleep
Julie takes out a book of word puzzles
And completes one after another
She laughs about the best ones with Dad
They don't include me
I close my eyes and seek out traffic-free paths

I feel Dad's eyes on me
I open mine in time to see him wink
I smile and
He guns the gas
Finally, I'm here
I feel the difference the second my sandals touch
      the dirt road

Little pebbles find their way back into my shoes
And I don't kick my feet to get them out
I inhale
It's only here
I can really breathe

| Summer |

Julie

~ The Lake House ~

Word around the lake houses is that Kyle and Alex are coming in two days. Their grandparents are psyched, making and buying all their favorite foods. Katie and I are by the creek behind the cottages again, skipping stones in the moonlight. It's what she does when she has Alex on the brain.

Katie is smiling as she throws another stone across the water. She closes her eyes and puckers her lips. What is it like to have a boy so gaga over you? Alex doesn't even know the real her. I mean, he thinks she's Miss Perfection, Miss Purity. Well, he better hold on to that sash, because Katie is not that perfect. Someone perfect would not chase boys that her sister likes—especially not Derek, my first kiss. Yep, one day he was tripping over himself to kiss my lips; a month later, the GPS went haywire and directed his lips to Katie's.

I thought he'd be different. I thought *she* was different. I mean, she helped me get ready for him, gave me her favorite lip-gloss. For what? I wonder if that's why she kicked extra high when they called his name on the court. Not for me, like she pretended, but for her.

I don't play pretend like Katie. If Derek stuck around long enough, he'd have seen the *real* me. I wouldn't act all sunny sunny happy happy if I wasn't, like Katie always does— moping, and then playing Miss Sunshine when she puts on her cheerleading skirt. But I guess that's what he wants. All the boys back home want that. They want perfect. They want a Katie. Not even a Katie, *my* Katie.

"Yulya," Katie calls from the rocks, "throw stones with me."

She skims a small rock on the water and it plops-plops-plops across in perfect little circles and splashes. My rock doesn't create delicate sprays. It lands in the water with a big splash.

"Try holding your hand like this," Katie says, gently turning my wrist and throwing the stone with me. Two plops, small spray. "See?"

"Yep." I jerk my hand back too roughly, throwing her off balance. She slips and cuts her toe, and it bleeds into the water.

"Shit, Julie. What's wrong with you?"

"I'm sorry." I didn't want her to fall. It was an accident. Wasn't it?

Katie

My toe is throbbing. I look away as it bleeds into the creek.

"Sorry," Yulya says again, but I can tell she thinks I'm overreacting.

"Forget it." I make myself look back at the water. I love how clear the creek is. It just absorbs the blood, and it's fascinating how it diverts it in all directions, thinning it out. Not like the chicken blood at all.

Yulya glances at me. "You're okay, right?" she says. This time her voice sounds worried and very much just-turned-fourteen.

"Yes, hon. Fine." I pat her leg in reassurance and she exhales. Sometimes it's so hard to read her. There are moments she's so young, looking for approval from everyone, jumping up and down because a boy she likes says hello to her. Then there are other days where she's hard, impenetrable; where her eyes flash spurts of hate in my direction.

"I'm doing it!" she shrieks, the sweet Yulya coming back. She throws the stones on the water like I taught her, like Sasha taught me right before he kissed me for the first time. I was almost fourteen, and he was my first kiss ever. Perfection.

"Grr!" she screams, throwing a pebble hard at the creek in retaliation for missing a skip.

I stifle a laugh, knowing if I don't, Yulya will lash out at me.

She slumps down on the grass.

"I can help you practice anytime," I say, and lie down beside her.

She doesn't say anything, then quietly, "Maybe."

I hear a car rumble down the gravel path outside and hold my breath. I know Yulya hears it too.

She snickers. "They wouldn't come so late. And anyway, if you miss him *sooo* much, why do you play your stupid games?"

I pluck at the grass. "What games?"

Even in the darkness I know she's rolling her eyes. "Oh, please. The not-talking-to-him during the year. It's ridiculous."

"It works for us."

She laughs. "Yeah, whatever. And only using our Russian names here."

"That's what everyone's grandparents use. Makes things less confusing."

Yulya backs down. "I guess." She finds a rock in the grass and tosses it into the creek. It sinks. "But," she says, turning back to me, "I still think the no-contact thing is stupid."

I hear the unspoken *so there* as she lays back down and crosses her arms. So fourteen.

Of course she doesn't understand. She's just like my mother in that way, thinking everything is so easy for me. Everyone wants Katie, so how could her life be bad? To my mother, my sister, my father the double life I lead may seem like lies, but not with Sasha. Our agreement leaves the world open. And when I met him, it was *before*. So that's who he knows—Katya who's never been kissed. Who loves having that spot behind her knee tickled by his fingers. Whose body warms up at his slightest touch and stays warm all summer.

Not Katie, the girl who slept with her ex-boyfriend and his best friend and barely remembers it. Who walks down the halls each day wondering if word got out, if the whispers are about her. Who wonders if she'll have to spend more lunch periods kneeling on the bathroom floor, drawing on the stalls. Who was lured in by the pom-poms, by the pyramid, who would do anything to stay on top of it.

The girl Sasha knows takes control. She doesn't let herself be coaxed into doing things she doesn't want to. Katya stands up for herself while Katie keeps silent, jumping at every shadow, dodging unwanted touches.

Before school ended, Chris said he'd go away, stop following me, stop appearing like a magician's trick each time I turned around, stop cornering me when the halls were empty and copping feels because he could. It was easy—I just had to sleep with him again. Sober this time, though, so I'd remember him. So I did, crying the whole time while his stupid dog licked my toes again. He told me he wouldn't move his dog; it was there first. Then, it was done. And he kept his promise. Those last few weeks of school, I was able to walk the halls in peace.

"Can you believe I'll be in high school next year?" Yulya asks suddenly.

"You've come to the basketball games."

Yulya props herself on one elbow. "That's not the same."

"High school is a let-down," I say.

She waves her hand in the air. "Don't patronize me, Miss Cheerleader." Then she's huffy again, all friendliness gone.

"Didn't meant to," I say gently. "I'm sure you'll love it." I try to pack enthusiasm into those words, use my fake cheerleader lilt to convey the year will be a *W-I-N!*

She laughs, I'm sure in spite of herself. "I know that voice," she says. Then, in Yulya style, she jumps up and raises her arms in the air. "*Gooo* East High! Yeah!"

"There you go. That's the spirit."

She collapses back on the grass in a fit of giggles. We do East High cheers and crack ourselves up. Flashes of my trees on the bathroom stall get fainter and fainter.

The sounds of cars swoosh by. The creek water laps on the rocks.

Our laughter gets louder, pushing that drunken night—Chris, Ethan, the blanket over my naked body—to the hidden places in my mind.

Kyle

Your grandparents—Babushka wearing the blue apron your dad once got her, and Dedushka in one of his checkered tees—run out to meet you, big smiles, arms open wide as Alex's car inches down the path. His honk, the first notes of "Shave and a Haircut," was your dad's signature, too.

They barely give Alex a chance to turn off the car before they're hugging you and taking your bags and ushering you in with commands to sit and eat and gain some weight back. They don't say anything about your mother not feeding you right or taking care of you properly, even though it would be their right and the truth. Their main concern has always been keeping things warm and good and normal. Even the wallpaper in the kitchen—bright orange and green flowers—is the same as it always was.

The lake house was their idea. They knew Katie and Julie's grandparents back in Russia, and when they reconnected in the Catskills, what better way to keep the friendship going than to see each other every summer? You remember how ecstatic Dad was. He said it reminded him of the vacations he took as a kid. He came every weekend. Sometimes your mom came too, though usually not. "This is the life," he'd say, parking his chaise longue by the wet laundry hanging on the clothesline outside. You and Alex would get the kiddie chaise longues he bought you and place them beside his. The wet sheets on the line blew in the breeze. There was always a breeze.

In the early mornings the three of you and your grandfather would set out, buckets in hands, and go deep into the forest to pick berries your grandma would turn into fruit punch and jam. You were eight the last time you did this. Your remember your father shielding his eyes from the sun, grimacing and smiling at the same time. You remember Alex acting goofy, throwing berries up in the air and trying to catch them in his mouth. You don't remember what was talked about, but you remember lots of laughing. When you think about that day now, the laughing hurts.

That fall, your dad found another man's boxers in the wash and moved out. You wondered what that would mean for summertime. Would you still visit your grandparents? Would the men of the lake house pick berries? You shouldn't have wondered. Three months after your ninth birthday, before summer came, he was gone.

Your mother—of all people—was the one who told you. She used her calm therapist voice because she'd earned her online degree two weeks before. "Now boys," she said to you and Alex, who would be turning eleven that weekend. He hated your mother for cheating and called her a "skank," mostly behind her back. She cleared her throat, looked down at the hot pink index cards fanned out before her, the open textbook on the chair beside her. "Now boys," she said again. "Something has happened, and before we discuss it, I need you to know it's not your fault." When she said this, you didn't think she was talking about anything that had to do with your father. You thought she was talking about Art, your possible stepdad. You hoped, even though you felt guilty for hoping, that the next words out of her mouth would be, "He's leaving." You thought of ways you'd make her feel better, like with a hug or peanut butter and jelly sandwich with strawberry jam—her favorite. Then, while she ate it, Art forgotten due to the jelly's deliciousness, you'd call your dad and tell him Art was out of the picture. You would convince him to come back home and give mom another shot. Funny choice of words in retrospect.

In the middle of this fantasy, your mother said, "Your father was a sick man. He had many problems." You didn't know what that had to do with Art leaving, and it confused you. Your brother banged his fist on the table. Hard. His eyes teared up, something you'd never seen before. You were still confused, but Alex seemed to know what came next. Your mother didn't look at him, was careful to only look at you when she said, "Boys, I'm so sorry. Your father ended his life today. In his bedroom. With a gun."

You stared at her, and all you could think about was that game Clue you were so good at, where Professor Plum killed Mr. Boddy. In the parlor. With a candlestick.

She turned over an index card. "I'm so sorry," she repeated. But she didn't cry. Your mother who cried at every sappy chick flick and infomercial, who just the day before cried when she saw one of those adopt-a-stray-dog commercials, didn't even tear up. She put a hand on your shoulder and the fingertips of her other hand on your brother's shoulder. "I'm here if you want to talk," she said, and glanced at the textbook on the chair before adding, "Can you tell me what you're feeling?"

Your brother shrugged off her hand and ran to his room. She sighed and turned to you. "How about you, Kyle? Do you want to talk? I want you to remember it's not your fault. He loved you." Her eyes were still dry, and you hated that. And you didn't understand why she thought you would blame yourself. Your dad would have been in the house with you had it not been for Art.

You shoved her hand off your shoulder and tried to think of bad words you heard Alex use. Then you looked at her, the snot from your nose collecting on your upper lip, tears dripping off your chin, and said, "I know it's not my fault. It's yours for being such a fucking skank."

The summers were different after that. Despite the attempts at normalcy, berry-picking was the one thing your grandfather couldn't do anymore. The main things you remember about that first summer *after* was absence and emptiness. And playing cards with Julie. When you were with her, your hands moving at the speed of light, you had no time to think of anything else.

Alex

Katya is at the lake, just like Grams said she would be. The orange one-piece she's wearing is soaked and a little see-through by her boobs. Last year, her hair hung down to her fine ass. This year it's cut short to her chin. I normally hate short hair; something really butch about it. But on Katya it's sexy. The sun shines down on her as she pulls her bathing suit away from her body, like girls do to stop the clinginess. Only she pulls it too far out and I see more than she'd want. I see everything. It's at this moment that she sees me and waves and runs to me, almost slipping on the sand, jumping on me, wrapping her wet legs tight around my swim shorts. I grab her ass, right there, in front of all the old farts watching us. The old men cheer, the women whisper, waving their fingers at Katya. She lets go quickly, her face red, like she forgot where we were or something.

This is the Katya I love. Or whatever that word means. This crazy Katya who doesn't talk on and on about separate worlds and shit. I never know what she's talking about when she goes off like that, but I always look at her all thoughtful, like I get it. Look at her mouth open and close, the tip of her tongue running over the top of her teeth when she's trying to make a point, and work really hard to hear what she's saying without thinking about the places on my body that tongue has been.

It would be easy to zone out when she starts getting all deep, but I feel I owe her something. I don't know why. Maybe it's because she's not like any girl I've ever met before. That's a freaking cliché, I know, but that's the best reason I can come up with. She's not a ho, or stereotypical Jersey girl with the long, painted fake nails, tight jeans, and sprayed hair. Hell, Philly girls are more Jersey than Katya. And she never wanted labels—unlike the skanks back home who ask for a commitment after spreading their legs on date two and claiming they've never done it before, all the while moaning like porn stars. Like anyone would respect their loose asses.

That first summer we hooked up, we saw each other every day, almost 24/7, and still we didn't screw. I'm not a complete asshole. I knew I was her first kiss, and I don't pressure (real) virgins. But she wanted to "do something special" for me, so I taught her how to jerk me off. She was good at it, too. When that summer finished, I didn't plan on seeing her again, not until the next summer anyway—if I decided to come back here. But I know how girls think, the shit that runs around in their heads about commitments and crap.

So I had my speech all prepared. I would tell her she was a great girl, really special and everything, that this summer would always mean something to me, like Kid Rock says in that song Katya loved, but things get crazy during the year, we lived too far apart. Hey, we could still IM if she wanted and be Facebook friends or something.

But she didn't give me the chance to say any of it. The last day there, while her parents were loading the car, she walked into my cottage, grabbed my hand, pulled me into the bedroom, and sat on my lap. Then she put her hand down my pants, rubbed me until I came, and kissed me hard. She smiled at me. "I hope to see you next summer," she said, squeezing my hand before letting it go and walking to the door.

In that moment, I believed she *was* special. Why didn't she want to exchange emails? Why hadn't I paid more attention to our fucking conversations?

"Don't forget me," I called as the screen door slammed shut.

Katie

My teeth chattering, goose bumps rising on my arms, I stand on my tiptoes and whisper in Sasha's car, "Let's get out of here." I pull him far away from the lake houses.

I'm thinking of warmth, of his arms around me, of our bodies colliding somewhere out of our grandparents' vision. Our usual spot—the first place we kissed—is the creek. Behind the willow trees, blankets on us, no one can see what we're doing. We've never made love, but we've come close. He's never pressured me, always said he wanted to wait and make it special. I used to agree, giddy at the idea of the *first time*. I imagined planning a date and circling it with a big pink heart on my calendar. There would be music and flowers and stars above us. Right before we did it, he would lean in real close and whisper, voice full of feeling, "I love you so much." It would be this special summer moment, like all those songs about romantic summers.

Then I met Ethan.

I didn't forget Sasha or what we had planned. I just thought of Ethan as my school boyfriend. I never thought of sleeping with him. I liked doing a special cheer for him at halftime, my fingers pointing at him. I liked the gaggle of cheerleaders following me, staring at me, like I could spread my magic *The Couple* fairy dust on them. Maybe I should have left more magic for myself.

"The grandparents are at some Bingo-athon," Sasha says now, stopping at his cottage. "Kyle's at the arcade." He extends his hand to me, like I'm still a princess, and I follow him inside, pulling at my bathing suit along the way.

"I've missed you," I say, falling onto the bed. He tosses a T-shirt and shorts my way and turns around while I change, like seeing that would be too intimate.

"Me too." He gets on top of me, and he feels stronger than before, or maybe I've just forgotten. I like his muscular chest weighing me down, his chiseled arms pulling me closer. His hands go under my shirt and I pull him closer to me. Then he kisses me deep and pulls my clothes off, and I panic.

Not that he hasn't seen all of me before, but his moves and kisses feel more urgent than I remember, his hands more insistent, and I think, *Our first time can't be like this. Katya and Sasha's first time is supposed to mean something. I don't want this right now.*

He's panting but can tell I've become a statue. He pulls back. "I'm sorry. It's just been so long. I want you so much."

He lays his head on my chest, mumbling more apologies, telling me he'll wait until whenever I'm ready. He wants everything to be perfect.

When Sasha talks like this, it's so easy to forget that this body of mine has already done it. And there weren't any stars out that first night. Chris didn't even have glow-in-the-dark ones on his ceiling. That first time wasn't real, anyway. The other time with Chris wasn't, either. Those times weren't perfect. They weren't with Sasha.

We start kissing again. This time he's more gentle. This time I'm the one who pulls him to me. I want him, too. I want his weight, his arms, his body imprinted on mine to block out the others. I move my hand to him to finish him off, and he tugs at my hair.

"You're so beautiful," he says when I'm under the covers, in his clothes again, goose bumps gone.

"You too," I say, running my finger along his eight-pack. I trace shapes on his abs and chest, asking him to guess what I'm drawing. We always play this game after. Usually, he guesses wrong.

"A heart?" he tries, after I've drawn a cat.

"You think I'm that boring and predictable? That *girly*?"

"I like girly," he says, getting on top of me again, kissing me deep and hard on the mouth, pulling the shirt over my head once more.

I'm digging my nails into Sasha's back and pulling at his sweat shorts when the door opens and Kostya walks in.

"Shit, asshole. You don't bother knocking?" Sasha yells, throwing a blanket over me.

I freeze again. Exposed again. But I remind myself that this isn't Katie's life. It's Katya's. And it's safe here under the blanket, in Sasha's arms. I manage to give a small wave. "Hey, how's it going?"

Kostya stutters, stumbles, backs out of the room

mumbling a bunch of *I'm sorrys* before slamming the screen door of the cottage.

Sasha flops down on the bed, fuming.

I put my hand on his arm. Despite Kostya being the same age as me, he oozes innocence. He's not like Chris. Not like Ethan. He didn't mean it. "I'm fine, okay? You can relax. Not like he planned this or anything."

Sasha doesn't say anything, and I squeeze his arm. "You saw how embarrassed he was. I bet he's never even gotten past first base, right?"

For some reason, he laughs. "He sure looks that way, doesn't he?" And for some reason I get goose bumps again.

Kyle

When it all started years ago, you were ten and Alex twelve. He thought he was so big because he was in seventh grade but already wrestling and playing football with the eighth graders. He liked to say that he could get more ass than most of them—which you're pretty sure meant heavy hooking up. Back then, that kind of talk impressed you, even though you didn't get all of it. The day it started, you and Alex were on the floor of his room playing Mario Kart on the Wii. Alex's flavor of the week, a curvy fourteen-year old—you think her name was Deedee or Deirdre or Daisy, but Alex always called her D—was on his bed making dumb comments. She kept asking him to play with *her* buttons instead of the controllers'. "I'm worth the wait, babe," he told her, not looking at her, not taking his fingers off the controller. Then he elbowed you and smirked, and you laughed like you totally got the joke.

You beat him three times. Fair and square—Alex would never throw a game. He punched you in your arm a little too hard—you had a small bruise the next day—but you knew he respected you. He would have punched you harder had you lost. "I'm done," he said, getting on the bed with D. She was wearing one of those shirts that looked like a kerchief, and Alex put his hand on her exposed stomach, right above her bellybutton ring.

"You can stay and keep playing if you want," he told you, sliding his hand further up under her shirt. You felt funny staying, but D didn't seem to care. She just giggled when Alex tickled the skin on the underside of her arm, and she grabbed one of his arms, around the biceps.

"So strong," she said, flirty, in awe. D was a freshman in high school, since Alex thought dating anyone in middle school was beneath him. He'd started lifting after your dad died and had the beginnings of a six-pack happening. Back then, you still wanted to know his secrets, you still wanted to know how he hooked himself all these chicks.

D giggled again, and when you turned around to look at her and Alex, you saw that her top was up by her collarbone. You'd never seen a bra on a girl before, just on mannequins. No one in your grade even had anything to put in a bra. You couldn't help but stare. It was pink and lacy, with little hearts all over it. You were afraid Alex was going to get mad at you for staring, so you got up to leave, but he grabbed your arm. "If you leave, you'll miss your turn."

You stared at him, face hot.

"C'mon," he said, smiling. "She doesn't bite."

"I sometimes do," D said, giggling. The giggle made you more uncomfortable.

"You gotta learn sometime," Alex said, and then pinned

D's hands down. She laughed and protested and you couldn't tell if she was really into the game or not.

"Aww. He's shy," she said. And that was when you saw she *was* into it. So you sat on the bed, but it was weird. Really weird.

"Go ahead. Touch her," Alex said. He still held down D's arms, as if she wasn't a willing participant.

Your hand shook as you slowly moved it to the bra. You laughed nervously, and the laugh sounded geeky. Like the kind that kid in your class had, the one who always wiped his nose with his sleeve and then inspected the snot like it was treasure or something. You didn't want to be that kid. That's why when Alex said, "Give them a squeeze," you did it, even though D didn't look as willing as she did before. But she squealed, "Alex, you're so bad," and laughed.

And when Alex finally let her free, imprints of his fingertips visible on her pale arms, she just ruffled your hair and said, "You just got to second. Congrats, little dude." And you knew you should have been happy and thought it cool, but you didn't. You felt nauseated and embarrassed.

So you looked at her, said "Thanks," and walked out of the room as fast as you could, ignoring the squeals and laughter behind you.

Julie

S pit," says Kyle. We're both straddling a bench, there's a pile of cards in front of us, and he's looking oh so cute with his dark, spiky hair.

I cough up a loogie and coat the dirt under our feet, and he laughs. Then, I take a card from the smaller pile of cards in my hand and toss it into the center. He does the same, his left dimple winking at me as he does it. Has he always been this cute? Sure makes Derek easier to forget.

Spit is all about speed. We grab cards and match our pairs quickly and lunge for more. I can usually wipe the floor with Kyle. Today I'm distracted. My hands move fast, but not fast enough. I grab for cards at the same time as him and hope our hands touch. Those few seconds of hoping cost me the game.

"Julie, girl," he says, when he runs out of cards first, winning the round, "you're out of practice."

"I guess we'll have to play everyday, then," I say, trying to be flirty.

"Sounds like a plan." He smiles, and I search for its meaning. But what do I know about reading people? Derek used to smile at me a lot. I thought I knew what it meant. Thought he wanted me. Turns out I was just a placeholder for Katie. One day he smiled the same way at her, and she ran away with it.

I wrote this in my journal after I saw their kiss, and Mama read it. Not only did she read it, but she waited for me in my room, the maroon notebook opened before her. I froze when I saw her, and she greeted me with her icy smile. "This is how you feel? That Katie stole him? Really?" She pointed to the notebook, no apology about reading it, no made-up story about how she stumbled on it while cleaning, just looking from the notebook to me. Her blue eyes were bright and eager like she really wanted to know what I would say, like we were in the middle of an argument, not me walking into an ambush.

My backpack cut into my shoulders, and I took it off and put it on the carpet in front of me like a buffer. Yes, that was how I felt. Why else would I have written it? But her eyes— same as Katie's—bore into me, daring me to say something else. I shrugged. "That's how I felt then." My voice was shaky.

She nodded. "And now?"

"I don't know." I stared at the shaggy, baby blue carpet. Katie was jealous when the roof leaked and the first carpet in my room had to be replaced. Hers was old, too, but still holding up. I wanted burgundy carpeting, and not fluffy. I wanted Berber—or a cheaper imitation version—so when I walked across it, I didn't sink in and forget where I was, so I could always feel the hardness of the floor with each step. But decorating was always Katie's and Mama's thing. They loved sitting in the living room with a clutter of open furniture catalogs around them. Katie's dream room was baby blue "bury-your-toes-deep-within-carpet." And, unlucky for her, the carpet in her room did not grow mold.

"The thing is, dear, it's not your sister's fault that boys find her attractive." Mama smoothed a stray hair and tucked it inside her hair clip.

I knew I should have kept quiet, but I couldn't help it. Derek was different. Derek had that smile. Derek kissed me. "Derek was mine," I said, in a voice that reeked of whininess and desperation. My mother hated that smell.

"No, honey. That's just the thing. He wasn't." She shook her head, smile still on her face, pitying me.

"So, what? He was Katie's then?"

She thought for a moment, picked a piece of lint off her sweater. "Well, he was more hers than yours." She said it so simply, so matter-of-factly, that it almost made sense. But it didn't.

"I need to start my homework," I said.

She nodded and got off my bed, leaving my journal open. "You know…" she said, when she was at the doorway of my room and I was on my bed. I sat in the same spot she was in seconds before, trying to reclaim it. "It would do you well to take responsibility once in a while."

"For what?" I didn't even realize I'd said this aloud until she answered.

"For who you are. We can't all be the pretty ones. You should find something else that lures them in."

Now, sitting across from Kyle, I know I still haven't found

that special power that brings in the boys. I can dive, thanks to my dad, but no one cares about that. And Mama doesn't like that skill anyway because it means I have to wear a bathing suit. I can play a mean game of Spit. Or I could, before I started trying to get Kyle to notice me. I stare at the piles of cards between us, forgetting what to do.

"Your turn," Kyle says, his foot kicking mine. "Wake up, Jules."

As he says this, Katie and Alex come up beside us. "Room for two more?" she asks, cocking her head to one side, giving Kyle a flirty smile. She's being extra nice for some reason, and her tone sounds, what? Apologetic? I can't quite figure out her expression. But Kyle blushes. That look I know; that look I've seen.

"Sure," says Kyle. "Julie keeps falling asleep anyway." He gives me a teasing smile. Then he smiles at Katie too, but that smile is shyer.

I smile back. "Oh no, I'm awake now." This will not happen again. "Wide awake."

Kyle

It's night, and you want to be alone and head for the swings but your brother and his girl are already there. You're wearing a dark sweatsuit and hope you blend with the darkness, but then they spot you and you have no choice but to wave back and continue forward.

"Hey, shithead," says Alex.

"Hey dickwad," you answer.

"Men," Katie says, laughing, throwing her arms in the air.

It's her arms, now covered in a turtleneck sweater, that you try to focus on because if you don't you will just keep picturing her naked and you definitely don't want that. So you just stare straight ahead and pump your legs and soon you're tearing through the air, heading for the trees, leaving all of them behind.

Julie

I don't look behind me when I leave the lake house. I only follow the sound of the swings. Okay, I'm lying. I look behind once—just once—because I'm hoping to see Kyle. If I saw him, I'd slow my pace and try to play coy. We had that word on this year's vocab final, and it sounds more sophisticated than "shy." Kyle seems like the type of boy who'd like the word coy. So, I'd play all *coy*, and tilt my head to the side—Katie style—and say, "You into swinging?" Then I'd toss my hair and smile that smile—*the* smile he only saw on my sister.

But I don't have the chance. Kyle is already on the swings with guess who beside him. And they're both soaring through the air at the same time, legs at the same height like freaking synchronized swimmers.

I hang back a few feet and stare as Kyle takes the lead, but he's not there for long. Alex is standing behind Katie and pushes her hard and fierce, like he needs her to reach Kyle. Like it's a game and he's losing. So typical of boys. I join them when Katie is finally caught up, and it's then she yells at Alex to stop pushing.

"Hey," she says, beside me now. She smiles and bumps me with her swing.

"Hey," I say, smiling back.

Then I pull the swing back and push off. I keep pumping my legs faster and harder until Kyle and I are at the same level. Until Katie, Alex, and the dirt below me are nothing but dust.

Alex

Fucking Julie kicks up a shitload of dust as she takes off, and now my eyes are watering. What is it with girls and swings anyway? Katya once said something about them being an escape. From what? If you have a problem, just deal.

Of course, it figures that my faggy brother is even higher than the girls. I get the speed part of it. Hell, I'd give them props if it was just about the speed. If it was just about how fuckin' quick you could move your legs. But it's more than that. It's like they're possessed, their faces blank like fuckin' ghosts. Looking at them is scary as shit. That's all I'm saying.

Now they're done swinging, and Kyle is back to staring at nothing. I bet he's trying to get Katya's boobs out of his head. I feel bad for the kid. If she was some whore back home, I'd have let him cop a feel by now, put him out of his blue-ball misery. But Katya isn't a ho. Simple as that.

Julie, on the other hand, would be good for Kyle. Not that she's a hoochie either, but she's one of those chicks who will do anything to be wanted. He wouldn't have to work too hard; it might up his confidence. I'll have to tell him to hit that later.

Right now, though, all the pussies are tired, and it's my turn to soar. I grab an empty swing and pull it back. "Watch how it's done!" I shout as I slice through the air. I'm faster than any of them were. I'm higher. The stars raise their palms and give me some skin. They are my bitches. That's how fucking close I am.

Katie

Yulya and I used to be close
I'm the one who taught her to touch the stars
To pump her legs, quicker, stronger, faster
To force the swing higher and higher into the air
And then lean back, her hair flying behind her,
Her voice a delighted squeal
The world upside down and rushing past her

These days, she acts like the swings are torture
I drag her there at night, hoping
To talk, to figure her out, to understand what I did
    that broke us apart
To find that moment when I stopped being the girl
    she could fly with
And instead became the one she wanted to fly from

Tonight I gave up
I took Sasha instead
He, at least, didn't put up a fight

But he didn't sit beside me either
"I'll push you," he said, not waiting for me
    to answer
Just pulled the swing back, back, back

And then let go
Not giving me a chance to look behind me
As I flew, flew, flew
Alone

Kyle

You knock on the screen door to Julie's cottage like you always do, even though it's wide open.

"Let's go, Molasses," you say. Your mother use to say this to you and Alex back when you were in pre-K, before the shit hit the fan. Funny that you remember it now.

"Sorry," says Julie, out of breath as she runs to the door. She's wearing a yellow towel over her bathing suit, so all you can see are green straps. "I'm wearing my new suit." She rolls her eyes, and her voice is shy.

"And what? You couldn't figure out how to get it on? Straps on top. You got it."

"Ha ha." She gives you a playful shove and then walks in silence.

What's with the awkwardness? You can't figure out why she's acting weird. You and Julie are what's easy. You never have to think when you talk to her—not like with girls.

"Uh, so, you want to see it?" she finally says.

You're about to joke and say something like *As long as I don't have to show you mine*, but she looks so nervous and unJulielike that you just say, "Sure." You throw in a smile, hoping it will calm her down.

She blushes and takes off the towel and you don't know what you're supposed to say, but know she's expecting something. You guess it's nice—all green with a little pink bow at the top. The bow makes Julie look like a little girl.

She quickly rewraps herself in the towel, and you know you waited too long to speak.

"You don't have to say it," she says. "I know I look like an idiot."

"No, it's nice. Really." It is. It's a decent bathing suit, but this complimenting thing is more Alex's gift than yours.

She shakes her head. "It's stupid. My mom made me get it. It's one of those suits—a Waist-Away or something—that's supposed to make you look skinnier. Whatever. At least I talked her out of the one with the skirt attachment."

Skinnier? You never thought of her as big. You never really noticed her body in *that* way at all. That was the best part of being with her. You got to just *be*. No pressure. You feel her eyes on you again, and the last thing you want to do is upset her. She's the best friend you have here. "The bow is nice," you manage.

She bursts out laughing, but it's a real laugh, and you're relieved.

"Don't even," she says, catching her breath. "I told my mom it was *not* 'feminine.' Just makes me look five."

"Nah. Seven easy." You both laugh.

"Thanks a lot. You wait until I whoop your butt at the lake. We'll see who's seven."

"Oh, then you'll look nine, ten even!"

"Ass!" she shouts, giggling, trying to hit you, but you run to the lake.

You meet at the dock and you both stare at the water. She raises her arms above her head, readying herself to dive in. Her brows are furrowed in concentration. Her face looks so serious. What can she be thinking about? Can't be about diving. That's easy for both of you.

In thirty minutes, the grandparents will start streaming in with the little kids who will be all over the lake and not let you race. Alex and Katie will wander in and cuddle in their special corner, but you know Alex will be watching you, too. Julie puts down her arms and starts fiddling with her bow.

You want Julie to smile so everything can feel good, so you can breathe in the easiness you two have.

"Hey, check it," you say, and do a cannonball into the lake. You know it's one of your better ones. You surface and see puddles everywhere. It even wets the nearby chaises longues. Julie is grinning, and you're glad.

"Oh yeah?" she shouts. "Check *this*!" Then she screams, "CANNONBALL!" and jumps in.

Julie

The water is cold and not in a good way. I stay underwater, open my eyes, and swim toward Kyle. It's like that game Shark we used to play as kids, like a water tag. I'm the shark this time. I swim close to the bottom of the lake and grab his ankle.

When I surface, I expect him to say I'm being babyish, but he doesn't. "You better run, girl," he says instead. Then he dives underwater.

I swim away from him, laughing the whole time, which makes the swimming harder. I feel giddy and silly and the weirdness of him seeing me in my bathing suit is gone. It's times like these—well, not only these times, but especially these times—that I'm glad my mom is not here. She'd freak seeing me play with Kyle like this, acting so young and dorky. I'd say, "I can't help it. Must be the pink bow."

I crack myself up and choke on the water and start gagging like the geek I am when Kyle grabs me at the waist. I swear his fingers are like magic because the gagging only becomes a small cough. He surfaces and sees my teary eyes. "You all right?" he asks.

I nod. "Choked."

"It's just a game," he teases, and I can see him trying not to smile.

What is this to him, I wonder. How did one school year change him so much? Why do I like him like *that*? And does he feel *anything* toward me? Anything at all? He's Katie's age, after all. Thank God she has Alex. I'm safe as long he doesn't dump her, too.

I cough again and Kyle whacks me on the back. I feel like a moron. In the movies we'd be looking into each other's eyes right now. Or dunking each other, *then* looking into each other's eyes.

Then we'd kiss. I stare at him and lick my lips.

"Julie?" he says quietly.

"Yeah?" I move closer and lightly touch his arm, like I've seen Katie do with Alex.

He glances at my hand and tenses. Or maybe I'm imagining that. I put it back at my side just in case. I think he exhales.

We continue to stare at each other and I hear little kids by the shore. Suddenly, Kyle splashes me. "You're it," he says, and swims away.

Julie

~ The Chickens ~

There are benches in a semicircle at the far end of the lake houses beside the dumpsters. Some grandmas lined the grass with newspapers to catch falling chicken guts, and now they're seated and waiting for the chicken man to begin. He gets out of his truck—white with a big yellow chicken painted on the side—and sets up the cages full of squawking chickens a few feet away. The grandmas get up from their spots to inspect and pick a favorite while Chicken Man sharpens his knives.

"Have fun," Katie says, scurrying away to join Kyle on the swings, her favorite place and also the furthest from the slaughter.

They never watch, but Alex and I always do.

"It's just sick," Katie says each time she sees the truck coming down the gravel path toward the cottages.

"Please. You eat it after Babushka roasts it. What's the difference?"

I'm sure in Katie's head, it's not the same. Just like she can have a school boyfriend and a summer boyfriend. She has this way of grouping things—"compartmentalizing" them, my English teacher calls it. Not seeing the killing somehow changes what happened, I guess. Maybe she decides the chicken my grandma cooks is not the man's but from the store (although those had to be killed, too, so whatever).

I don't think I'm sick for wanting to watch. It makes me feel better, like I can somehow give these dying chickens support before they're sliced. Like a last request before the electric chair. And then there's a part of me that just wants to watch because I know it bothers Katie.

Today, Chicken Man is wearing a nametag: *Wilbur*. The only thing I can think about is Wilbur from *Charlotte's Web*, and that's just wrong. If I were him, I'd opt out of the name tag.

"Wilbur," laughs Alex, coming up behind me. "Talk about ironic." He swings a leg over the bench and sits down beside me.

"Look who finally learned to read," I say. I don't know what surprises me more   that he knows the meaning of irony or that he's read *Charlotte's Web*.

He raises his eyebrows. "Watch it, little girl, or I'll have to spank you."

He looks like he might actually like to do it, and that grosses me out. I move away from him, and Wilbur picks up his first chicken. The knife slices and blood splatters all over Wilbur's clothes, face, and hair. He curses and drops the chicken. It flies over the other chickens, leaving its blood on their feathers. The grandmas grimace.

I glance over at Alex. He looks fascinated. This chicken is a fighter, and he likes that. I don't know if I do. What's the point in fighting if you know, in the end, it won't help. Just better to go quietly and not ruffle any feathers.

The chicken is not finished and more blood flows from it. Finally, it lands at Wilbur's feet. Who would want that chicken now? It's hot and I swear I can smell the blood. My stomach rumbles and I think I'm going to be sick.

"Shouldn't stick around if you can't hack it," says Alex.

I want to punch him. I swallow down the vomit rising in my throat. "I can hack it."

And the look he gives me is weird, like I fascinate him, like he'd like to see what I would do if I were the chicken.

"Huh," he says. "Maybe you can teach your big sister to be tough."

Me teach *her* something? A strength I have that Katie doesn't? I like that. I clench my fists and bare my teeth. "Maybe." Wilbur pulls out another chicken and I face Alex. "Bring it," I say.

Alex

Today is chicken day, and I'm pumped.

"How can you watch it?" Katya asks as she heads to the swings.

The real question should be, how can you *not* watch it? It's *Survivor, Real World,* and straight-on documentary all rolled into one.

I'm not some sicko (but no worries, I've been called worse) who gets his jollies watching headless animals flail around. It's just something to do.

I jump over the bench and sit next to Julie. Today Chicken Man got himself a name. "Wilbur," I say laughing. "Talk about ironic."

"Look who finally learned to read," she says. Wouldn't surprise me if *she* secretly gets off on watching Wilbur wield his knife.

"Watch it little girl, or I'll have to spank you," I say, knowing this will skeeve her out. She plays it so innocent but I wonder if she's the type who'd be into getting paddled. Not that it matters, since I'm with Katya. Besides, she's more Kyle's speed. He needs someone like Julie who doesn't know a guy's cock from his balls. A girl who knows what she's doing freaks him out. I've been watching the two of them in the lake, playing tag like lame-asses. How is that kid sixteen? If it were me, there'd be no swimming away.

Wilbur takes out his knife and starts slicing away. The first victim is a feisty one. They usually aren't. When the knife cuts the chicken's artery, severing its head, blood splatters in Wilbur's face and hair. I laugh, and everyone stares at me but I don't give a fuck. That chicken deserves some respect. It's fighting it out, trying to show ol' Wilbur that it ain't going quietly. It flies high in the air over the other chickens, raining blood on their feathers. Take that, bitches! You're next. See you in chicken heaven! Wilbur curses, and the chicken is losing steam. It lands on Wilbur's bloody shoes. Some feathers fall to the dirt. He picks it up, puts it in a plastic bag, and gives it to a grandma, tossing the head in the green dumpster behind him.

Julie looks like she's going to hurl. "Shouldn't stick around if you can't hack it," I say.

She swallows. "I can hack it," she says quietly, a fierceness on her face I've never seen on Katya's.

"Huh," I say. "Maybe you can teach your big sister to be tough."

She clenches her fists when Wilbur pulls out the next chicken. "Bring it," she snarls, like this is what she's been waiting to hear.

Her eyes flash fire and hate, and I'm glad Katya is not here to see it.

Alex

Three weeks since the chicken man came, and nothing has changed. Same old shit. The grandgeezers play cards and dominoes all day. The clothes make the same sound on the line outside: *Thwack. Thwack. Thwack.* At the first sign of gray clouds, the grandmas take down the clothespins and rush the clothes inside. Sometimes I wish for a surprise thunderstorm just to shake things up. If it weren't for Katya, I'd lose my mind. Doesn't hurt that we still haven't done it. I save that for the sluts back home. I don't want Katya to become one of *them*. They get me off, but they're growing stale, like we're one fuck away from growing mold.

The saddest, most pathetic shit of all here? Kyle and Julie. One of them needs to grow a pair soon and I'm putting my money on Julie. I'm watching Kyle from the window now, playing another game of Spit. He's not even trying to touch her. She puts her cards in a pile, leaves her hand in the middle of the damn bench, and I can see she wants him to touch her hand like in those dumb-ass chick flick movies. It's embarrassing, really. For all the game Katya has, Julie has nada. And I don't think it's the age thing, because I had plenty of game by the time I was fourteen.

So she finally moves her hand after my loser of a brother picks the other pile. The bigger pile. Which makes me wonder if he didn't go for that one on purpose. You'd think the kid could get play any time he wants with his pretty boy looks— dark hair, god-given athletic build (shithead doesn't even have to work out), even has a fucking dimple in his cheek. Maybe he just thinks she's a woof. Sure, she's a little on the chubbo side, but it's not something puberty won't fix. And the thing is she knows she's chubbo and those kinds of girls, they think they're not all that, so even when they thin out and get hot, they're still thinking they're nothing. That's why it's good to get them now so they think, "Wow, he liked me back when I was all fugly and shit."

But Kyle doesn't get that. Holy fuck, she's leaning forward now, her tits almost in his face, and he's ignoring them. Jesus. It shouldn't surprise me, I guess. Even when we do our thing and I let him share, he's not that into it. He swears he's straight. So I guess he's just a pussy.

Like before we came here, there was a girl—Sarah. Totally into him, totally wanted his shit. Not who I would have picked for him, which I told him. Which he ignored. If I were choosing, I would have picked the girl who lived next door to us: cute little thing, black hair down to her tiny shoulder blades, not much makeup except for pink gloss. Instead, he chose this girl with "natural" bleach-blond hair. Natural my ass. Wore jeans with a hole in the knee, shirts that fell off the shoulder. Fuck, she had *slut* written all over her. "Don't talk about her like that," Kyle whined. "She's cool. She reads poetry. She's into Dylan Thomas." I didn't care if she published her own damn poetry book, the girl was a whore and how Kyle didn't see this or care was crazy.

He ignored me every time I tried to bring this up. Just took out the damn controllers and started on the Wii. Then, the day before he brought her home for the first time—the only time—he snapped. Threw the controller across the room. "Shit, Alex, can't you just let it go? Just because all your girlfriends are hos doesn't mean Sarah is. Okay?" I didn't bother answering him. Just left the room. What was the point in arguing, when I could just show him.

The day he brings her home, Mother Dearest decides to be Super Mommy. She'd broken up with her guy du jour and spent the week watching sappy chick flicks. This always transforms her into one of those fifties moms—the ones who actually pretend to like their kids, who ask about their day, who wear clothes that cover their tits and cooch (when they're not doing their stripper gig, anyway).

"Hi, honey," she said, apron-clad, voice smooth as Cool Whip, when Kyle brought Sarah home.

"Hi, Mrs. Miller," said Sarah, smiling, extending a hand to our mother.

"Well, aren't you sweet? Can I fix you kids something?" Mom asked, and I rolled my eyes. The way she said it would make anyone think this was how our house functioned, like our mother wore that stupid-ass *Something's Cookin'* apron every day, like she gave a damn about us on a regular basis.

I would have told her to fuck off right there, but Kyle

bringing a girl home was an event in itself. He smiled at my mom, playing nice for Sarah's sake. "Sure, Mom. Whatever's good."

"Oh, baby," she said, laughing, "everything's good."

Kyle clenched his fist by his side at this, and I coughed a little too loudly. I mean, who was she kidding? More than half of the food in the fridge was past expiration. That's why we had enough take-out menus to wallpaper the kitchen. Anyway, while mom busied herself in the kitchen, Kyle took Sarah to our room. Since it was Kyle, I figured they'd just be playing video games for the next half hour, but when I got upstairs, I saw them dry humping, her hands rubbing his back, her eyes closed while he kissed her. They didn't see me and I waited until Kyle finished and went to use the bathroom. Her shirt was still unbuttoned when I walked in and she scrambled to pull herself together.

"Hi," she said, blushing.

"I'm sorry. I didn't mean to interrupt." I said this all gentleman-like.

"No worries," she said, brushing her hair from her face and sitting up on the bed.

I sat down next to her, real close. So close that I smelled her cheap-ass perfume. Same perfume the last whore I was with wore. Lust or Flirt or something like that. I put my hand on her knee, and she didn't move it away.

I leaned in next to her ear. "You know," I whispered, "you can read all the poetry you want, but that's not going to keep your legs closed."

Now she moved to the other end of the bed. Fast. Her face went white. "I'm not like that." She said it quietly.

"Maybe not now, but you're like that. Trust me."

She stared at me, her eyes tearing. She sniffled. A tear fell down her cheek.

Damn. I hate it when girls cry. Only bastards don't have weak spots for that. "Hey, hey," I said softly. "Don't do that. Look, I'm not judging. You're not a one-guy-at-a time kind of girl. More power to you. I just don't think that's what Kyle needs." I tucked a strand of her hair behind her ear. I smiled at her.

She smiled back, uncertain. I leaned in, kissed her. Her body went all rigid but she didn't move away. "See?" I said, pulling back, leaving her looking confused, embarrassed, guilty. "Cheating comes naturally, doesn't it?"

"Oh my God! Oh my God!" She just kept repeating that, and then jumped up, ran to the door.

I grabbed her hand in the hallway, just as I heard Kyle coming back. "It's okay to be a whore," I whispered. "Just don't pretend you're something you're not."

She snatched her hand away and ran, Kyle calling after her. I tried explaining that I did him a favor, but he wouldn't listen to me. Ungrateful shit.

Kyle

Hanging out with Julie has stopped being easy, now that you have to monitor every move, wonder about every touch. An arm around her isn't playful anymore. You find yourself stopping, thinking too much. You're not clueless, like Alex thinks. You know how girls act around guys they like. You know what Julie is doing. You just don't want it.

The sky darkens, and she talks about going to the swings. Her voice is hopeful, and you have to squash the hope. "I'm tired," you say, which is true. You're tired of Spit. Tired of avoiding Julie's fingers each time she lingers on a pile. You're tired of losing the game because you're too busy watching her hands and where they'll go before you commit to a pile.

"All right then," she says too quickly, like she's trying to be noncommittal. "Rest up. We have a Spit rematch tomorrow." She hesitates for a minute, like she's waiting for a hug. You used to say good-bye with hugs. You almost reach for her, but that would give her the wrong idea. "Later," she finally says, and gives a small wave before running into her cottage.

You feel regret and relief. Then from behind you hear,

"Nice work, pussy," and there's no more relief. Just regret and fear.

"Leave me alone," you say, but when has Alex ever listened? You turn your back to him and head toward the creek. Your dad once showed you how to skip stones on the water. Today you want to make up your own rules. You focus on distance, on the biggest splash. You feel Alex behind you and don't turn around. You grab a rock and this time you hold it tight. You feel it dig into your palm and it's all you can do not to heave it at Alex's head. Anger radiates in all directions, and it's like in comic books where the hero is surrounded by an invincible bubble. Your bubble is red. You squeeze your eyes shut and push the anger down. The bubble lightens to yellow but it's still there. You hear his breath behind you and try to calm down. For yourself, not for him. He has enough power over you. He must sense you're not you, must sense something is off, because he waits to speak until you've let go of the rock and slumped against a tree for support.

He lights a cigarette, takes a drag and blows smoke in your face. "So, what is it?" he says, like we were in the middle of a conversation. "Does she not give you a hard-on or something?"

"I like her as a friend."

He looks at you like you just ate dog shit. "What the fuck is that supposed to mean? You've known Julie for years, been hanging out with her every day this summer, and you like her 'as a friend'? Are you ten?"

The orange tip flickers as he takes another drag. You don't like smoking. The smell makes you sick. But when he offers you a drag, like he always does, you take it. Like you always do.

"She's nice. That's what I mean." But you know he won't let this go. What are you supposed to tell him? That even if you did think a girl was pretty, there's no way in hell you'd tell him? That dating someone close to your age, dating in general even, makes you want to throw up and you don't know why?

He blows smoke rings and then spits on the ground, and this makes you think of Julie and you smile.

"Nice?" he says, and your smile is gone just like that. "That's all? Well, you can fuck nice, can't you?"

When you were younger, you thought he was God. Maybe not God, but someone like that, someone important, someone big. He was all you had after your mom gave up on being a therapist and connecting with you through index cards. When she decided ten was too old for hugs, when she thought she looked too young to be anyone's mom, and instead hit the gym to get back the body she claimed she'd had before she met your dad. She tried to get back that life, too, and it didn't include you and your brother.

But she didn't just leave you. That would have been better. She was still there, sometimes cooking meals, usually leaving cash for delivery men, all the while looking for something better. And you knew it. With each want ad, each informercial, each outfit that looked like it belonged more on the girls your brother brought home than on a forty-year-old woman, you knew. So you had Alex and he watched out for you and you thought he was right. You thought you owed him. But as time went on, and he called you fag, and pussy, and hit you a little too hard, you started to hate him.

Then there was Sarah. You didn't think she was everything. You didn't know what she was. But she stopped you from being numb. Kissing her made you less scared. And Alex can claim she wanted him all he wants, but you know she liked you. Not that it matters. Not that she'll ever talk to you again. All because of Alex. After that, your hate for him grew stronger. So that's where you are now. Hating him, in the woods, with him and his putrid cigarettes, hoping he will just shut the hell up. But he doesn't.

"Shit, kid, all the girls you kissed were on my coattails. Except for Sarah. And she was definitely *someone's* sloppy seconds." He pauses. "And thirds and fourths too."

He laughs, and you're in the red bubble again. This time it's harder to talk yourself down, and you're not sure you want to. The woods turn red. You aimlessly throw the rock. You hear shouting and pick up more rocks and keep going. Then it's just black and pain as your arm is twisted behind your back. His breath is right by your ear. "Are you fucking crazy?" he asks. "You could have hit me."

Now you laugh. Did he think you cared if you did?

He pins your arm tighter to your back, and it's just you and him in the woods. No colors, just pain. "Are you done, psycho?" he asks. The pain is bad. You nod and he lets go of your arm.

"What the hell was *that*? I was just trying to help. What are you going to do when I move out and can't look out for you anymore?"

Fucking celebrate. "I don't need you," you say quietly.

"Please, little brother. Who the hell else do you have? You think mommy dearest is going to pull a Julia Roberts and bring home some millionaire daddy who loves her for her soul?"

"Babushka and Dedushka are here."

He laughs. "How long do you think it will be before they kick it? And they only have us for the summers. Face it, I'm all you've got."

Your throat goes dry as the truthfulness of that sinks in. Sometimes you think your mother cares, but she's too busy trying to bring in money any way she can to see anything else.

He watches your face, amused, knowing he got you. He takes another puff of cigarette and moves in likes he's going to punch you, but at the last moment moves his hand and combs his fingers through his hair. "Psych," he says, laughing.

Julie could be someone else who's there for you. She could be a way to freedom.

"Fine," you say, "I'll ask Julie out." The words come out thin. You don't want to ask her. You don't want to ask her because of *him*. Why does everything have to be on his terms? How did that happen? Why do you still let it happen?

"Well, bravo." He claps real slow, like in the movies. "I think I see a ball," he says looking at the zipper of your pants. "But word of advice? It's summer, asshole. You don't need a whole production. Just grab her, give her some tongue, and don't worry about a relationship."

You're quiet as the red surrounds you again. You know right then that he'll fuck everything up. Just like he did before.

"You still there?" he asks. When you don't say anything, he gives you a cigarette.

You inhale deep and feel the burn in your lungs. You hate it but do it again. You need the burn. You need the pain. That's the only thing that feels in your control right now. You inhale again and again and again.

Katie

Mama is here for a three-day weekend and making my life hell.

"How can you live here, Katie? It's so ... so ... primitive." She frowns.

"That's the appeal, and it's *Katya*."

She waves her arm at me like I'm a bug she's trying to swat. It grazes the sticky fly-catching paper hanging from the ceiling and she shrieks. I bite my lip not to laugh. "Primitive," she mumbles.

"Why did you come?" I swear I can smell Jersey on her.

She looks at me like she hasn't heard me right. "To spice things up for you. Bring some civilization back." She holds up her cell phone proudly.

"It won't work here. You know that." I take it from her and show her the little line through the phone. "See? No reception." Thank God.

She pouts. "And here I thought I was doing you a favor. Figured you could text your friends. I'm sure I could drive you somewhere with email."

That's the last thing I want. "I'm fine."

She shakes her head. "You can tell me the truth— Babushka is outside. We're the same, you and me. You need adventure, the buzz. The phone ringing, the parties. We don't do well when we're forced to blend into the background. I saw it after Ethan broke up with you."

I want to tell her I've been in the forefront of too much buzz. I want the background. Disappearing in the summer is heaven. She takes my silence for agreement.

"I just don't want you to make the same mistakes I did. And look where we are." She spreads her hands out to illustrate, but I know she also means Cherry Hill, not just here.

"What's so bad about where we are?" I ask it as if I really don't know. She needs to think we're alike, and I'm scared to tell her we aren't. Scared to tell her I haven't been fun, free-spirited Katie for a while.

"Nothing, if you never had more. But I almost did."

I know this story. The popular frat guy she lost because she stripped in front of all his friends after too much booze. Disgrace runs in the family. The thing is, she never told me this story. I heard her talking with Babushka long ago. I knew better than to tell her I knew.

"But you met Dad, so it all worked out." I want her to stop talking and leave. The phone, even though barless, is offensive on the bed. I feel Cherry Hill getting closer and closing me in.

She laughs bitterly. "Yeah, I guess it did. You father had no issue with the fact that I was rotten goods—" She catches herself and looks at me. "I never told you this, but I, um, showed some bad judgment. Details aren't important, but let's just say it made me lose the homecoming king."

"But you got Dad," I say again, stupidly.

She leans in as if there are other people around. "Let me tell you something. You're old enough to hear it now. Your father is a good man. Good husband. Good father. He provides for us, et cetera. But what does it say when someone is so willing to look past the spoils in front of him? He only cares about what's on the inside, he told me. You know what that shows? Desperation. Weakness. And I was weak too, and desperate for some kind of future, so I took it."

The images in the crevices of my brain get big again. *Shots, keg stand, me fading, Ethan on me, Chris, pushing, pain.* They spin around on a loop and won't go away.

Mama touches my hand. "It's a lot to take in, I know. I just thought you needed to know. Don't settle for almost. Don't be desperate, Katie."

Alex

I knock on the door of Katya's lake house, obviously interrupting some powwow between her and her mother. Katya looks spooked, and her mother waves me in. Don't know what it is about that woman, but I don't want to be on her bad side.

Mrs. Taylor smoothes her skirt and flips her hair. "So nice to see you again," she purrs. Whoa, wait. Is she actually flirting with me?

"You too, Mrs. T. And"—I test out my theory—"you lost weight, right? Looking good."

She beams and giggles. I sneak a peek at Katya, but her face is blank. She obviously has not recovered from whatever I walked in on.

"Thank you," says Mrs. T. Then she leans forward, bringing attention to her tits, which is something she doesn't have to do since those puppies are already hanging out. "You look like you've been working out yourself—doesn't he, Katie?"

I half-expect her to pull a cherry stem out of her boobs and tie it into a knot with her tongue. I'm game. Old bitches, young ones, I guess they're all the same. I flex my arm, and she flashes her too-white teeth. Katya finally snaps to and moves beside me.

"Sure does, Mama," she says, and makes a show of grabbing my biceps. She's smiling but still white as my ass. I wrap my arm around her waist and pull her to me.

Then the old bitch squeals like some girl at a boy band concert and lunges for my guns. "Ooh, let me," she says. "We old ladies don't get to touch muscles like that anymore."

Katya turns red. Shit, how did my Katya come out of *that* gene pool?

I play her. "Who are you calling old? If I were a few years older and not dating your daughter…"

"He's a charmer," she says. "Reminds me of someone I knew back in college."

Katya tenses, and, fun game or not, I don't need some beauty-queen has-been pissing her off. "Later, Mrs. T," I say as Katya squeezes the shit out of my hand.

"Oh please," she says with that whore giggle. "It's Anna."

"See you soon, Anna." I flex one of my muscles again, and Katya pulls me harder to the door.

"I was wrong a few minutes ago," says Anna, looking at us. "You definitely traded up, Katie. Don't let this one get away."

"It's Katya," she answers, and slams the door.

Julie

Mama came last weekend and Dad is here now. My parents say they like the one-on-one time with Katie and me; that's why they don't come here together. Mama spent most of her time with Katie, other than to tell me— after seeing me in the bathing suit—that she may have been wrong about the suit; green is not really my color. *What IS?* I asked. She thought for all of two seconds, then said, "Maybe you don't have a color." Nice.

At least Dad doesn't put me on edge. I don't really talk to him about boys, unless he asks. Usually, he doesn't. He never tells me I need to lose weight—but this could be because his middle seems to get rounder every day. Right now, it's right before dinner time, and the lake is empty and we're sitting on the dock dangling our feet in the water. When *he* saw me in my green monstrosity, he said the bow was cute. He's easy. He's nice. So why is it I only care about what Mama thinks? I once heard Babushka say that Mama's standards were crazy high. Maybe that's it. Reaching them will make me feel I have achieved something. With Dad, it's like those classes where everyone gets an A. Doesn't mean as much.

"How's your summer been?" he asks.

I shrug. "It's fine." Could be better, if Kyle would just look at me the way he looks at Katie. But he doesn't.

He doesn't actually look at her like he wants her, but it's this deer in headlights look. Like he's frozen by her. Why don't I have that effect?

Dad looks at me and splashes the water with his feet. "Just fine?" There's teasing in his voice. What does he know?

"I think fine is pretty good."

"Hmm," he says. "You and Kyle looked like great buds playing cards."

I'm sure my face is red. "We're just friends," I mumble.

"If you say so." He smiles and kicks a bit of water my way.

I wish Chloe was here. I don't talk to Katie about Kyle because it seems just uttering the names of boys I like sends them her way. And forget about talking to Mama, because she'll just say Kyle is out of my league and maybe she's right, but I don't want to hear it now. Dad is here. Dad won't judge. I sigh. "It's not me who wants to be friends," I say.

"How do you know *he* does? Teenage boys can be clueless."

Does he think I have a shot? It might get my hopes up.

"Well, he'd have to be a complete imbecile not to know. I've done everything the magazines say."

Dad raises his eyebrows in alarm, and I roll my eyes. "You

know, like, touching his arm ... " I trail off. The details are embarrassing. "Trust me, he's gotta know."

"Look, kiddo, men don't know much and boys even less. Unless you've said you like him—point blank put it out there—I wouldn't bet on anything."

I splash the water with my toes. I'm feeling better. "You really think so?"

"Yes, honey, I do. Give it a shot."

I smile at him. It feels good talking to him about this. Then he says, "It's how I got your mom," and that changes everything.

I heard about him and Mom. Not everything. Not all the details. Only that Mom thought she settled. She told me herself—not in those exact words, and not about him specifically, but about her life, and Dad is part of her life, so how else could I take it? Once, I saw her looking at an invite to her college reunion, and I asked her if college was fun. I don't know what possessed me to ask the next question, maybe I was just getting into boys, but I asked her if she'd had many boyfriends.

"There was a boy before your father," she'd said. "He was something. Now *there* was a strong guy." She didn't have to add, "unlike your father." I got that. After that, I watched Daddy more. Saw how he gave into everything she wanted. How he didn't argue with her over *anything*. It seemed ... weak.

"Yep," he continues as if I've answered. "And we've been a-okay. But if I'd sat back and said nothing? Who knows where we'd be today. Probably not here with you." He grins and ruffles my hair, and I feel guilty for thinking bad things about him.

What if he's right? Didn't going up to my mom—the homecoming queen herself—take guts? "All right," I say. "I'll tell him."

"Attagirl. And when he reciprocates, treat him good, okay? That boy is a good egg. I can tell."

Katie

"Hang with us tonight," I tell Yulya. She's lying on the bottom bunk reading something from her summer Required Reading list. She's seemed perkier ever since Dad was here, but not around me. Only when she's playing Spit with Kostya. With me, she's moody.

She doesn't look up from her book. "I don't think so."

"We're going to Wild West City and Sasha said Kostya is coming." This isn't true, not yet. But I want her to come. She was so unhappy at home, and here, too. I thought summer at the lake houses would snap her out of whatever funk she was in this year. It hasn't, but the arcade—the arcade with Kostya—could help.

She doesn't put down her book, but she stops moving her hand mid-page-flip. "Yeah?" There's excitement in her voice, and I can also tell she's trying to keep it toned down, hoping I won't notice.

"Yep." I climb down from the top bunk. This could be my chance to get in her head. Kostya, huh? I suspected she liked him. He seems like a nice guy. But I thought Ethan was nice too. And Chris. And Derek. What do I know? My radar has obviously been defective. "Want to borrow one of my tops? Maybe that sleeveless pink cardigan you always stare at?"

"I do not," she says, finally putting her book down and smiling. Actually smiling. Her guard is disappearing, and I can almost see it happening, rolling down, down, down like a car window.

"Makeup?" I say.

"Are we on a makeover reality show?" Yulya asks, snorting.

I roll my eyes. "Hush. You're ruining a perfect sister bonding moment."

"Too perfect, no?" she says, but gets off the bed and walks over to me. She sits on the chair by our dresser and closes her lids so I can apply eye shadow.

I don't know when I'll get this chance again, so after the pink shadow, I add blush, and then lipstick. "Why didn't you tell me you liked him?" I ask as she admires herself in the mirror.

She shrugs. She never tells me anything anymore. Maybe she doesn't even know why.

"Well, he'd be crazy not to think you're beautiful." I toss the cardigan to her. "Put this on. I'll be right back."

I leave the room and run to talk to Sasha, stealing one glance behind me. Yulya is standing still, holding the cardigan to her chest, blush getting brighter, eyes getting dreamy, a look on her face I don't recognize. Happiness, maybe.

Julie

I feel pretty, and I am scared to let the thought grow. Once it's out there, it can be blown to smithereens. Back when Derek and I started our whatever-that-was, I thought it. That first time he kissed me, I thought, "Wow, Derek Santos is kissing *me*. I must look good." That could be when it all began to go to hell. Like being vain for that split second made everything unravel.

I put the cardigan on, leaving the top button open like Katie does. It's tighter on me than on her, but it molds with my skin and hides the pudginess. Wearing it makes me want to forget the last time I saw Katie in it. It was the last time Derek came over. I heard the door open and his voice downstairs and waited until someone called me down. I was wearing lipstick and blush and thought he'd swoon when he saw me. Minutes passed and no one called so I forgot about grand entrances and made my way down the stairs. He and Katie were laughing in the kitchen. I hadn't heard Katie laugh since Ethan dumped her and my first thought was, "Good. I'm glad Derek is cheering her up." But then I paused a few seconds on the stairs and watched. And he was leaning in so close, and I saw his arm brush hers. He smiled the smile I thought was meant for me alone and ogled the pink cardigan like it was a winding road and his eyes were afraid of losing course. I went back up the stairs and made lots of noise coming down. When I got into the kitchen, he wasn't leaning into her like that anymore.

We went for a walk, and I was so stupid. I still thought the walk would be romantic. It was a break-up walk.

Two days later, I saw the two of them pressed up against the side of the school, oblivious that anyone else could see them. I told myself it didn't matter. When she kissed him back, letting his hands roam over her like only his eyes did in our kitchen, I pretended it didn't hurt.

I kept waiting for her to say something or act differently around me. She didn't. It was as if nothing happened. Maybe to Katie, it *was* nothing. I mean, it was just another boy. Kisses came easy for her. So I stopped "overreacting," as my mom said. And kept telling myself he was never mine.

"Yulya, let's go!" Katie now calls from outside.

I glance at the mirror again and pat the cardigan like it's magic. A speck of gold glitter falls into my hand. I pocket it and run out the door.

Kyle

You could escape in video games for days. So when Alex asks you to come to Wild West City with him, Katie, and Julie, it's a no-brainer. You know Alex really wants a double date or double fuck or whatever he's thinking, but you pretend you don't get that part. You never did ask her out like you told him you would.

But Wild West City will be a good, neutral spot either way. When you and Julie were kids, the two of you took pictures there. The kind where you put your head on top of a cowboy or cowgirl body. Maybe you can do this again with her. Just have fun like you used to, before her hands began creating detailed plans to touch yours.

By the time you get to the car, you're feeling excited. You're going to show the pinball machines who's boss. Maybe even win something for Julie, like the good friend you are. But then Julie gets into the car, and she looks hopeful, and you feel like shit. "You look nice," you say, and it's true. She does. You're just being honest, you tell yourself, ignoring the way the hope reaches her eyes. She swings her leg closer to yours, letting her toe touch yours. It takes a lot but you leave your foot where it is even though you want to jerk it away and run.

Then you're at the arcade and you can breathe again. Alex and Katie tell you where to meet them and then leave to make out or play games or both. It's just you and Julie, her standing so close you feel her breath on your neck. Warm girl's breath. It brings back memories of Sarah, of Alex's girls, of what you never wanted and what you can't have, and you leave them and Julie behind. You search for air. You find Alex and bum a cigarette. He gives you four and punches you lightly in the arm like he's proud of you or something, like the cigarettes mean something. You punch him back and laugh when Katie tells you to keep the cancer sticks away from Julie.

You walk away from the noise of the games, away from the crowds, away toward the highway and just stand behind the barricade, smoking your cancer sticks and watching the cars whizz by. It's easier to breathe here, where exhaust fumes are safe smells.

"Can I bum one?" asks Julie, suddenly beside you.

Your eyes were closed, and you were content getting lost in the rush of traffic. You take a few seconds to open your eyes, another few seconds to answer. "Sure."

"I've never done this before," she says with a nervous giggle, her fingers brushing yours when you pass her the cig. "You'll have to corrupt me."

"It's a bad habit."

"I can just do it once in a while, like you. I think this is the first time I've seen you smoke."

You think of talking her out of it, but who are you to do that? She wants to do it with you, and if you were a normal person, this would not be a huge deal—you might even be flattered that a girl wants you to teach her something, even something as vile as smoking, to get closer to you. You push that out of her head and just focus on Julie. Good ol' Spit-playing Julie.

Her fingers are shaking as she brings the cigarette close to her shiny pink lips, mimicking your motions. You teach her to inhale and exhale, talk her through the coughing, tease her about the head rush. She smokes half of one, and shyly asks if you can help her finish. As you do, your mouth covering the little pink ring left by her lips, she asks if she can have another few puffs. You let her, and there's something about the way her mouth covers that same spot yours was on that makes you feel light.

This feeling is familiar. It's the Sarah feeling. It scares you, but when Julie says she wants to stay out here a little longer and look at the cars with you, you say okay. And when she moves closer to you, her bare arm touching yours, the part of you screaming to get away is silent.

Katie

She likes him," I tell Sasha at Wild West City as we watch Kostya and Yulya from the hood of his car.

"No offense to your sister, but it's pretty obvious." He takes a drag of his cigarette and blows the smoke away from me. I don't like when he smokes in front of me, but at least he doesn't blow it in my face like Trina said her ex did.

"So Kyle knows?"

"My brother is socially retarded. I had to tell him." He flicks the ashes into an empty soda can.

"Interesting," I say, walking my fingers up Sasha's arm to his collarbone. "Does he like her back?"

Sasha laughs. "You girls are funny. You could've just started the conversation that way—I would have told you." He takes another drag. "I think he'll give the idea a chance."

The relief I feel when he says this surprises me. But it shouldn't. "Good. He has to. I kind of owe her."

"You, a cradle robber? Steal your baby sister's boyfriend or something?" He laughs like this would never happen.

"Sort of. He was in my grade, and he tutored her. They

hooked up and then suddenly broke up. He told me it was her idea. She didn't want to see him anymore..." I don't know why I'm telling him this. Maybe I think he'll tell me I did nothing wrong. He looks at me—at Katya—like she can do no wrong.

"So there you go," Sasha says, clearly bored. "Whatever happened wasn't your fault. What's with girls and drama?" He takes a long drag and then throws the butt on the ground.

It's so simple, the way he says it. But it's hard to know what's my fault anymore; what I wanted, what I didn't.

My fault: Ignoring the way Derek looked at me. There was a want in his eyes.

My fault: Believing I could be silly and flirty Katie again, like she wasn't gone.

My fault/not my fault?: Derek asking me to meet him after school. Saying he wanted to talk about Julie. I thought he wanted love advice or something. I should have known. He said they were over; he wanted me. He leaned in so close. I froze. He pushed his lips on mine and I didn't fight back. Again. He finally pulled away. Asked what the hell was wrong with me. What was with the frigid act? He'd heard different, he said.

I stared at him, afraid to ask if he really had or if he was just talking trash. I didn't even walk away. Just stood there like a mannequin. It was he who finally left, after calling me a tease. I don't know how much longer I stood there before I remembered I could move. I almost told Julie, but what would I say? Her first kiss wanted *me*? I wonder if she could see it in my face, though, when my mask fell off. I wonder if that's why she just turned cold.

"There's a girl code," I say now, focusing on the more clear-cut situation (more clear-cut to him, anyway). "We only kissed once, and then I told him it was wrong." *In my head. That's what I tell him each time I replay the scene. I move. I push him away.* "He was Yulya's—"

"He wasn't anybody's." Sasha pops a piece of gum in his mouth.

He can't understand this.

"It should have never happened, so now I just hope she and Kostya work out."

"You think too much," Sasha says, moving his hand to my cheek. "Don't worry about them. I'll help make it work, okay?" He gently lifts my chin, moves it close to his mouth. It smells of minty gum. I like that gum. It leaves that sharp, cool taste in his mouth, taking away almost all traces of ash.

I kiss him, and he pushes me down on the hood of the car, pins my arms behind my head. Flash: *Ethan holds my arms above my head with one arm while he strokes my side with the other. It will be okay. Sshh.*

But then Sasha's breath is near my nose, and I breathe it in deep and I'm back at the car. Back under his weight. I let him take control. I melt into the car and escape.

Julie

- The Chickens -

It's three days after Wild West City, and Wilbur's truck squawks down the gravel path.

I put on my flip-flops and pull a pair of shorts over my bathing suit. "You coming?" I say to Katie. I know she won't, but I like watching her reaction when I ask. Always a look of disgust. But today, she doesn't answer no right away. She actually seems to consider it.

"Would it be weird if I came? Like, do you and Alex have a vibe going, doing some play-by-play or something?"

I shrug. "I don't know if you'd call it a 'vibe,' but yeah, sometimes it's a cool spectator sport."

"Why?"

I hear the truck squeal to a stop. The squawking gets louder, and I know he's taking the crates out. They're going to start and I'm getting antsy. "I don't know. It's something to do." I think about it more because I know she wants a better answer. "Sometimes I like to see which one fights the hardest."

"Why? Does that make it taste better?"

"Geez, Katie. I don't know. Why the sudden interest?" Cages rattle. They're starting. "In or out?" I ask, almost at the door.

She sighs. "Tell Alex I said 'hi.'" Then she opens the back door and heads to the swings.

"Sure," I call out. "You do the same with Kyle." Because I know he will be there, too. And for some reason, knowing that both of them hate Wilbur bugs me.

Alex

Julie runs to the bench just as Wilbur grabs the first chicken's neck.

"What took you so long? Chickening out?" I crack myself up.

"That's a good one," she says, rolling her eyes and doing an exaggerated slap on her leg. "No, your girlfriend was actually thinking of getting in on the fun."

Girlfriend. Does Katya call herself that? I don't do girlfriends. But… "Oh yeah?"

"Looked like it was actually going to happen, and then she, uh, chickened out." Julie laughs. She's wearing that stupid green suit again. If it weren't for that, she'd actually seem a little cool.

Wilbur slices the first chicken's throat quickly. She barely squawks. Just falls right to the ground. He's getting better.

"Impressive," says Julie. She fiddles with her bow, and it draws attention to her tits right below it. The summer's feeling her. She's tan now, and some chunk has moved from her waist up to her boobs.

She takes her eyes off Wilbur and catches me looking. She raises her eyebrows. And something hits me then. She doesn't believe in that same shit "code" that Katya does. I could hook up with her, and not only would she do it, but she wouldn't tell Katya.

Not that I would. I save my player mojo for the Philly whores, not Katya. But I store the info anyway.

A chicken flies over our heads and I duck as blood sprays. "Fuck," I say.

Julie doesn't even squirm, just looks toward the swings. What the hell is wrong with Kyle? If I was his age and there was someone as willing as Julie—and I can tell she so is—I'd be all over that. Shit, I'd even be all over it now.

"What's with your brother?" she asks, quietly, as another chicken falls to the ground. Wilbur curses as the blood squirts on his chin.

"He's a pussy," I say.

"Maybe, but he always has stuff to talk to Katie about."

I laugh. The thought is just too stupid. Like Katya would ever go for Kyle. "Probably because she doesn't put the moves on him."

She looks at the swings again. "I guess."

"Seriously, little girl. You have nothing to worry about." I grab my dick. "No girl can pass up on this."

Julie laughs and rolls her eyes. "Puh-leeze."

I don't tell her I'm fucking right about my dick. That's why they all keep coming back. But we're back to the chickens and done with the girl talk.

"Make you a bet," I say. "Next chicken flies only as far Wilbur's kneecap."

"You're on," says Julie. "What are we betting?"

"I win, you buy me a pack of cigarettes. You win … " I watch her fiddle with the stupid-ass bow again. "You win, I give you a few bucks for a hot swimsuit."

"Done," she says.

Wilbur grabs another chicken out of a cage. This one's a fighter. It flies out of his hands twice before he captures it for good. I'm losing respect for good ol' Wilbur. He can't control that hen at all. He only gives her a small cut and she flies out of his hands again.

"He's pathetic," I say loudly. Wilbur gives me the finger and grabs the hen with new gusto. Yeah, asshole, you showed me. Tool. The next slice is clean and takes the head off. Another chicken would have dropped dead on the ground. This hen flies.

"C'mon," whispers Julie. "Past the knee, past the knee."

Fuck me. This hen is going to do it. I could have used a new pack of smokes. She flies to his chest and then collapses. "Yes!" Julie says. She starts yammering about the kind of suit she wants. She's talking about something like Katya's.

"Sure." I yes her to death, but I know what she's thinking. That the suit can make miracles. I mean it would be an improvement over the crappy one she's wearing, and she's getting hotter, but it will never make her look like Katya.

Wilbur points to his eyes, then to mine. Like he's watching me. He raises his thumb in the air all proud of himself. What the fuck for? He barely kept her down. If it were me, that bitch would have never stood a chance.

Alex

Katya and I head for the creek, blanket, picnic and cheap wine in tow. I even bought pink plastic wine glasses so they matched the strawberry wine. I thought Katya would get a kick out of that, but she keeps eyeing the wine, all nervous.

I don't do picnics. I don't do slow. But for her, I want to. What's up with that? And what's up with that sour look on her face? I grab her and put her on my back, piggyback-style, and she squeals in surprise.

"Giddyup!" she says, giggling, grabbing my ass.

"Oh, it's like that, huh?" I grab her ass with my palms and squeeze and she laughs as we run down the hill.

We sit on the grass and throw rocks into the water, watching them jump and shit. I open my backpack and take out two peanut-butter-and-jam sandwiches and pink napkins.

Katya smiles. "Nice touch," she says, pointing to the napkins. She takes a big bite out of the sandwich. There's jam on the side of her mouth and she brushes it away, embarrassed. The girls back home don't care about that shit. They'd just keep chowing down like pigs and open their mouth to show the evidence, too.

"Anything for you," I say, and pull her to me and kiss her on the cheek.

I pour wine into a cup, and she looks at it like it's poison. I guess I was wrong thinking she'd drink. Doesn't everyone? But this is Katya. Maybe she's a Puritan or something. No sex, no drinking. That may be a little much for me. "You don't drink?"

She looks sick, like she just downed three bottles all by herself. "I haven't in a long time."

"Badass hangover or something? I've been there."

"Something like that." She nibbles on the sandwich.

Maybe she was stupid drunk the last time. Lost it and showed someone her boobs. The idea makes me laugh out loud and she looks at me like I'm crazy. There's no way she would do that, but I've seen a lot worse. Maybe she just lost control. Some chicks don't like that at all.

"Hey," I say, my voice soft because her eyes still look spooked. "It's okay. It's just you and me, and you'll be totally safe. I promise."

She relaxes a little, looks around like she wants to make sure I'm not fooling or something. "Promise?" she asks, and her voice sounds younger than Julie's.

"You know it," I say. "I'd never hurt you." I've never said those words before, let alone thought them. I feel around my mouth with my tongue, trying to see if they really came out of me.

She looks at me, her eyes big. "I believe you wouldn't. You're not like all the other guys."

And I feel like a shit, because I am. Just not with her.

She finishes her sandwich, licks each finger while staring into my eyes, and drinks the entire cup of wine.

"Whoa! Hold on there, killer," I say when she starts to pour herself another. She grabs the bottle away from me and pours another cup. I lunge for it, but she chugs it down before I can stop her.

"I can hack it," she says. This should disgust me, this lush party-girl act, but it doesn't. Maybe because her eyes look scared.

I play along. "Oh yeah?" I pull her down to my lap.

"Yeah," she whispers. She leans her head against my chest and picks up a pebble. She throws it into the creek, and it skips twice. I do the same, and we stare at the creek for a few minutes, just throwing pebbles. Katya takes the bottle of wine from the dirt, swaying a little, then stares me in the eyes like she's daring me to stop her. I don't, and she chugs down more than half the bottle.

"I told you I could hack it," she says, then kisses me deep and hard.

I push her down on the grass. She claws at my chest and jeans and then she's on top of me, her hand working double time inside my jeans. I cup her boobs through her shirt, and she moans.

I want her so bad, and she looks at me like she knows I'm about to burst. She reaches for the Boone's and chugs more. Then she's back on top, kissing me harder, moving her hand faster.

"Jesus!"

She moves her mouth down, and I'm so close.

She stops.

"Don't stop," I say.

"Don't you want to be inside me?"

Oh my fucking God. Those words are so hot, and I want that. I turn us over so I'm on top and fumble with the buttons on her shirt.

"I wantsh you to," she says. "Please." She moves my hand to the zipper of her jeans.

But she's slurring her words now, and her eyes are not there.

I catch my breath. The parade of whores flash before my eyes, and she's not them. "Not like this," I pant.

She moves my hand between her legs. I pull it back. "Why? You a virgin?" she murmurs.

If she only knew. "Not for a long time," I say.

"Then why not? I'm not as innocent as you think."

"You're innocent enough. I'm not fucking you while you're bombed."

"We'll see," she says, pushing me off her. Gets on top of me again.

Fuck. This is so fucking hard. I'm so fucking hard. She's rubbing against me, and I explode.

"See? You have all that power without even screwing me."

"But I wanted to," she says quietly.

"I know, baby. Me too, but when we do it, it will be when

you're sure and sober. I'm not going to be that asshole who needs to get a girl wasted so she'd fuck me."

She moves close to me, and suddenly she's crying. Oh hell. "I'm not what you think I am," she says between sobs.

Oh geez. Is this because she hooked up with Julie's ex? She's been talking about that more, since Wild West City. I've seen a lot worse. "You're what I want."

She shakes her head. "Not if you knew me. The real me."

I get it. This is the Philly-Jersey shit. Well, I don't want to hear it. "Katya is all I need to know."

She's passing in and out of consciousness now and mumbling things.

"What's that, baby?" I ask.

"Two people," she says. "Have you ever done it with two people?"

"Like two girls?"

"No," she says, all sarcastic. "With two guys."

"I thought that what happens in Philly and Jersey stays in Philly and Jersey," I say. "It's a good rule." I thought it was a stupid-ass rule when I first heard it—to the extent she wanted to keep the worlds private, anyway. But I don't like where this conversation is going, and I'm more afraid of whatever the hell she wants to reveal about herself than telling her anything about me.

"Aw, c'mon. I just want to know more about the real Sasha." She shifts her body and moves her hand south. I move it and place it on my stomach.

She doesn't want to know more about the real me than I want to know more about guys she's hooked up with.

"How about we start with baby steps. You can start by calling me Alex, and I'll call you Katie instead of Katya. It will be like we're two different people." I wink at her.

"No," she says slowly, but I know she's not going to finish the thought. Her eyes close. She passes out beside me, and I stare at her half-naked body for a few seconds before rebuttoning her shirt and wrapping her in a blanket. With our grandparents in the cottages, I can't bring her back to them. So I lie down beside her and put my arms around her to keep her warm. Then I close my eyes and hope she won't bring up shit when she's sober.

Katie

"Fuck! What time is it?" I scramble to my feet and fall back down as the sun hits my eyes and the world spins.

Sasha looks at me, amused. "One bottle of cheap-ass wine is all it takes to get you trashed? Lucky me."

I smirk at him, but any movement makes the ground spin. "Shut up," I say, but not with much oomph, and then turn away from him and throw up. The trees and grass spin, and a world of green rushes at me. I throw up again. I've been here before. I shiver. I tell myself it's not the same. I'm with Sasha. Last night was fun. Nothing bad happened. *It's all good. It's all good. It's all good.* I'm dizzy again, and now covered in cold sweat.

"Just lie back down. I saw Julie this morning and she told your grandparents you got up early and went for a run. She was in a good mood."

I don't face him as I wipe the spittle from the corners of my mouth and the ends of my hair. "Disgusting," I mumble. "I told you I don't drink anymore."

"You're saying that like I made you. I tried to *stop* you."
He laughs.

I remember more. He stopped us from having sex, too.
Even though I threw myself at him. How did I get so lucky
with him?

"Thank you," I whisper. "For not sleeping with me." I
don't even want to look at him.

"No worries. Glad you're so willing, though." He winks at
me and kisses the top of my head.

"I remember you avoiding my questions, too," I say, still
facing away from him. Why do I bring this up again? To see
how far I can take it? To see if he'll run?

"Do you really want to know everything about me?" he
says to my back. "Do you really want me to know everything
about you?"

I shrug. I don't.

"You can't even look at me because you're afraid of what
I'll think of your puke breath. I think that's your answer."

"Speaking of puke, I should clean myself up. I'll see you
later." I get up, aware that I'm pouting. I stumble, and he
catches me at the waist before I fall.

"Let me know when the stink is gone," he says, laughing.
He kisses me on the cheek.

I walk up the hill slowly, my body aching. I say the name
Alex in my head. I whisper it so quietly I can barely hear it
myself. I taste how it feels in my cotton-mouth. It feels wrong,
bitter. And I know that Sasha's right. I don't really want to
know everything. And I can't let him know Katie either.

Julie

How was your run?" I ask, a little too loudly, when Katie walks in looking like shit.

"God, not so loud," she says. "Thanks for covering for me, though." She looks toward the shower but then shakes her head and crawls into her bed.

"Seriously? You're not going to clean that stench up? Babushka will smell you in the next room."

"I'll take care of it. Just need a few minutes." She pulls the blanket over her head. "How was your night?" she mumbles.

"Good."

We played Spit in his room and when his hand brushed mine, he didn't move it away. When it was time to go home, he walked me to the door because it was late and dark. But there was no hug or kiss. There *was* a lingering of his fingers on mine. I don't tell Katie any of this; I learned my lesson last time. But there's this blinking thought in my head, like those yellow lights that mean to proceed with caution. It's telling me he may have looked at me as more than his favorite Spit player, but not in the shy, stumbling, red-in-the-face way he looks at Katie. I try to shut off the blinking.

"Just good?" She sounds disappointed.

"No tonsil hockey," I offer.

"Sorry," she says and groans into her pillow. "God, I am so hungover. So if you don't need any sisterly advice, I'm going to crash."

"You have my permission to be a bum."

Katie's breathing deepens and I look out the window. Kyle is sitting on the bench by our cottage, playing cards in hand. He looks toward our door but doesn't get up. And he doesn't leave. I tap lightly on the window, and he motions for me to come outside.

Kyle

Seeing her makes you happy, and you hate that. Look at what happened the last time. Will Alex just let you be with her, or will he fuck this up like before? Will he test her too? You don't know if you're scared for yourself or Julie. Probably for both of you.

"Hey, dawg," she says sitting down across from you.

"Yeah, homie, what up?" you answer, laughing. She's so easy to be with. You shuffle the cards and make a show of letting her cut the deck.

"And spit," she says, once you've both chosen piles. You both spit on the grass at the same time.

Fucking lame-ass, you hear Alex say. *What are you, eight?* You push his voice out of your head, but it's been in there too long and has carved a spot in your brain. At last you get it to quiet down; not disappear, but it's better than nothing.

You play three rounds. You win all three, and that makes you feel confident. "Want to go for a walk?" you ask, and she nods, slipping her hand in yours. And the confidence is gone, just like that. Your legs become rubber, and you sweat. *Shit, why are you such a fucking girl?* You follow her lead and push your legs forward. She talks about going to Wild West City again, having a game-a-thon, and this relaxes you some.

"Alex ever teach you to skip stones?" she asks when you're at the creek.

"No, my dad taught me. Taught both of us." You grab a rock and throw it across the water. It bounces once, twice, three, four times. That was the last thing you and him did together before he left. He took you to the local pool, which was really a sandpit with water. It was one of those days that looked like it might rain, so the pit was empty. You spent an hour talking and throwing. He teased you and ruffled your hair. A week later, he found out about your mom and Art. Two weeks after that, he was gone. Less than a year later, he was dead.

"Wow, that's really good! Can you teach me?"

You gently move her fingers to cover just the tip of the rock and show her how to fling her hand. It takes a few tries but she finally gets it to skip. "I did it!" She throws her arms around you and you stiffen under her touch. *Pussy.* "Want to smoke?" she asks, and the way she says it, you know it's because she's grasping for something to do with you. She feels like she did something wrong—you made her feel like she did something wrong. Damn. Why can't you be normal?

"Sure," you say, and sit on the grass and look at the rocks and the fish swimming in the creek. She inhales deeply and then tries to do smoke circles, but coughs.

"Easy there, overachiever," you say, and bump her lightly with your shoulder.

She smiles and takes another drag. You do the same.

"So what was your dad like?" she asks.

You never talk about him. "He was a good guy."

"I remember him a little. We tried to teach him Spit once, right? I'm sorry he's gone."

"Thanks." You take another drag. "What are your parents like? I don't really talk to them when they visit." Funny that you've known her for so long and never thought to ask.

She shrugs. "I've seen better," she says, smiling.

You smile too and squeeze her knee. You sit in silence and wait for signs. *Just kiss her. Grow some balls already. That vagina getting dry?* You hate that it's only his voice that you hear. You hate that it's getting louder. But then she leans over and kisses you, and the voice disappears.

Julie

I hear the swings and know he's there. Call me crazy, but I can pick out which rattling of rusty swing chains belong to him. I wonder if we will kiss again tonight. If it will feel any different in the dark and cold than it did in the warmth of day. I haven't seen him since it happened yesterday, but that's fine by me. The first meeting after the kiss will almost definitely be awkward. Maybe having it take place by the swings where we can do something besides stare at each other is key.

I didn't tell Katie about the kiss. She might have asked me to explain, and I can't explain what is was like... kind of powerful, but held back at the same time. Does that even make sense? Like I could tell he was really experienced but shy, too. That's all we did, though. Just kiss. And it was nice. Nicer than with Derek. Righter than with Derek. But maybe that's in my head. Derek felt right at the time. And then became all wrong, all should-have-never-happened. That's the other reason I didn't tell Katie. I opened my mouth, even—was so close to telling her, and then she did this hair flick my mom does, her blond hair skimming the curve of her chin, and I couldn't do it. Couldn't have someone else tell me that another boy wasn't mine. Could never be mine. And what if Katie took Kyle away, too?

Maybe she knew, though. Maybe his lips transferred some of their pink to mine and made them extra shiny. She smiled at me and offered another cardigan. A purple V-neck, just as soft as the pink one. She wore a light blue sweatshirt and jeans, and looked beautiful because she was Katie. She kissed me on the cheek before she bounced away, her blond hair in tiny braids.

I put on the sweater and lick my lips. I didn't eat anything today. Chloe once told me she could totally taste her first kiss hours later. I wanted to see if it worked for me, too. I've probably licked off every trace of him by now. But then I close my eyes and run my tongue over my lips again, and I swear I can taste him.

Kyle

When you open your mouth, gasping the answer to Alex's question, you taste the mosquitoes in the air. They leave a trail of meat and blood.

He lets you out of the headlock and slaps you on the back. "Attaboy," he says.

You cringe. His touch always makes you want to throw up.

"Get a little titty action?" he asks next, hitting his new pack of cigarettes against his palm. First one side, then the other, then the first side again. Pound. Pound. Pound. You know better than to ignore him.

"Just lip," you say, backing away, bracing for some hate from his mouth or his fists. But he just shrugs. "Sometimes it's better when you drag it out. Keeps the suspense going."

"Sure," you say, wanting to get away. You're not even sure if you meant to kiss her back. You keep going back and forth on if you want it to happen again. You never feel in control anymore.

Alex lights the Marlboro Red, inhales deeply, and blows the smoke in your face. He grins and offers you a cigarette. You want it so bad, you inhale Alex's smoke. But you shake your head and walk out into the night.

Alex

It's cold as hell out tonight. Katya is wearing a sweatshirt but I can see the outline of her nips if I look hard enough. And I do. She's playing a lot tonight. Swinging then stopping, jumping off, running around, tackling me. She's just laughing and shit and not bringing up anything serious. I wonder if this is because of Julie and Kyle. If so, I'll have to be nice to the 'mo. Sometimes I think he hates me, and I don't get it.

Isn't this what big brothers do? Beat up on the little guy to toughen him up and hook him up with girls? Fuck if I know, but I wish I had someone around to do the same for me. It's times like these that I think about Dad. I remember shooting the shit with him. He'd take me fishing and we'd laugh at the small fish we caught. He never let me feel bad about not bagging a big one.

Once, I got real mad, though. Couldn't catch anything if my life depended on it. So after the trip, we went to this Korean fish place in town. Craploads of fish all on ice. They looked just like the ones in the water, only they were dead and cold. He told me to pick any one I wanted. I picked this grayish blue one, the size of my arm. Its mouth hung open and the eyes were popping and staring at me. We drove back to the lake and dad put a hook in its mouth and handed it to me. Had me stand holding it, like I'd caught it. He snapped a picture with his old Polaroid camera. He loved that thing. It came out right away and he waved the photo back and forth until the fish and I appeared.

When we got home, he bragged to Mom and Kyle about it. Showed them the pic and everything. Kyle was floored. Just stared, open-mouthed. I blushed. Dad put the picture on the fridge. Mom patted my head, but didn't say much. Why would she give a rat's ass about us when she had Arty by that point?

When Dad moved out, I wanted to live with him. I was going to tell him, but then he offed himself. Because of that stupid bitch.

"Penny for your thoughts?" asks Katya, corny as hell, but it makes me like her more. Want her more, if that's possible.

"No, baby, you don't want these thoughts," I say, getting behind her and wrapping my arms around her waist.

She rests her chin on my chest and leans into me. I put my arms under her sweatshirt and touch her bare skin. All I want to do is pull a Kyle and kiss her, nothing more. But she pushes herself hard against me. So I go for broke.

I bite on her ear, stick my tongue in there. Whisper that we should get out of here. And she agrees so quickly. Philly Alex would have thought *skank, whore, slut,* but Sasha doesn't think this way. Not about Katya.

"C'mon." She breathes hard, pulling me toward the creek.

I leave Kyle on the swings—he sure as hell doesn't care where we go—and follow Katya. Her fingers grip my hand tight, like she thinks I'll get away, but fuck if I'm going someplace else.

"Chill," I say, slowing her down. "The creek isn't going anywhere." I pull her to me and kiss her deep.

And when she kisses back, she sucks me dry.

Katie

The air shifts
and I feel the kiss lingering inside me
Parts of Alex being left within
I take his hands in mine
Put one to my cheek
His head nuzzles in my neck
His body
Goes limp
A whisper, so soft, so needy, "Katya."
Into the night,
my whisper in return, "It's Katie."
He raises his head
I bring my mouth to his
Tasting him
Stare at the stars above us
As he erases the past
And let him suck me dry.

| **Fall** |

Julie

-Cherry Hill, NJ-

A month into the school year, and Katie is different. Not the broken, mopey girl Ethan dumped last year. She also dropped the Katya thing and lets Alex text and email her. And she keeps an eye out for me at school—waving hello, stopping by my lunch table. I've almost forgiven her for Derek—who I have to see every day. But having Kyle makes it easy to forget him.

Kyle and I have been talking on the phone, and he seems lighter, too. I'd like to think it's because of me. But then there's my mother. She watches Katie and me like she's waiting for something to happen. Something to explode. I don't know if Katie sees it. She and Mom still do their powwow thing when I turn in for the night, or say I am. I don't want to hear what they're saying, so I don't strain too hard to listen. But their laughter can be loud. Sometimes it calls me, but it's more of a courtesy invite. I know better than to think it's really asking.

Katie

The thing with being happy is that it's easy to forget that my world once imploded around me. Like today, I get the pizza lunch and walk to my regular table. Everyone is huddled together, and Trina sees me first. She gives a quick wave, then starts whispering and gesturing like she's taking Miming 101.

Then I see Marissa's face and she bites her lip, totally nervous. What the hell? Did I wear the wrong cheerleading ribbons? I'm almost at the table when the missing link arrives. He parks himself next to Marissa, grabs her hand—I'll give her credit, she's trying to hold back and not flaunt it—and chows down on his slice. Moron that he is, he's oblivious to the girl stares around him.

"What?" asks Ethan. "Is there shizz on my face?"

Only nervous giggles, and I sit down next to Trina.

"Hey, Kate," he says. "Long time. Have a good summer?"

I search his face. Nothing there but hungry boy. How can he act like that after ... everything? I shiver, and the girls look at me with sympathy. They think I'm bummed because

Marissa is dating my ex. If it were just that. Hell, she can have him. They can make shallow babies together.

I take a bite of my pizza and channel his mind-erasing powers. I move the last time he touched me out my head and replace it with me and Alex. Our first time by the creek. The stars above us. Him so gentle, not doing anything without asking me first.

"Yep. You?"

He goes on about football practice and laps and his best bud Chris. I nod and fake happy while everyone basks in this super Brady Bunch family we have, where everyone gets along. Trina pats my arm, like she knows I'm just putting on a brave front. Which I am, but not for the reasons she thinks.

Marissa glances at me a few times and I wonder if she's scared I'll spill about her and Mr. Stevens. Is there *still* a her and Mr. Stevens? That would make for some good gossip.

I eat more pizza and watch the happy couple, their fingers now laced tighter together.

"It's meant to be," whispers Trina.

I stare at her. "What?" Then I remind myself she doesn't know. She's just caught up in this new high school drama, just waiting for me to throw down with Marissa.

"You know," she stammers. "It's not like you haven't found someone new, too."

I smile wide. "You're totally right." And the real happy starts coming back. It blocks out Marissa and her new molester boyfriend. I take out my phone and text Alex: Miss you.

A few second later he texts me back: You too, Katie.

And that name doesn't scare me. Especially not from him.

Alex

~Philadelphia, PA~

Look at you, working boy," says my mom when she sees me in my pizza-delivery getup. "About time you found something to do with yourself."

"Beats hanging around here."

"Ain't that the truth." She looks me in the eye, challenging me, like a big *fuck you.*

Screw her. But I don't say anything. She's in one of her moods, and I'm not in the mood to shout. It's easier dealing with her when she's all doe-eyed, in her *poor me, why do my kids hate me* phase. Then I can say whatever and get her bawling and leave. "But I've changed," she'd say. "Why can't you just forgive the past?"

Maybe I should. But life here was crap. Her pimps coming in and out. Smacking the shit out of me when they felt like it. I tried fighting back, but then they'd try going after Kyle and he was so small back then, so I let them beat me harder so they wouldn't get him. That's why I tried to teach him to toughen up, be a man. This world blows and you don't always want to be the one doing the blowing. Someone has to suck *your* dick once in a while.

Then, one day, it all stopped. Like, out of nowhere. She quit whatever shit she was doing on the side, got a job waitressing and stripping at a high-end place where bouncers made sure she stayed pretty. 'Cause, you know, who the hell is going to pay for a broken-down, beat-up stripper? She decided she was going to be Best Mom Ever. And it was like those years never happened. But I was thirteen already. I mean, Christ, how the hell am I supposed to just forgive? Forgive her telling me to "just take it easy" on the scum she brought home? Forgive her saying the smacks were my fault, that I should just learn to play nice because we needed the money? Fuck no. *Fuck no.*

"You getting home late?" I ask.

Right away she's on the defensive. "Why? You got something to do?"

I don't even know why I asked. Just making small talk. "No. I'll be late too, so leave Kyle some cash for dinner."

She snorts. "Can't you at least bring home free pizza? It can be my reward for letting you 'find yourself.'"

Whore. How the fuck am I ever supposed to leave this house if I don't have money? "He wanted Mexican today."

She curses, but leaves the cash.

"You're the best mommy ever," I say. "How did I get so lucky?"

"Watch your mouth, Alex." She raises her hand like she did this summer.

I laugh. Great empty threat, bitch. "Too bad you're done hooking, or you could ask one of your boys to do your dirty work," I say.

She goes pale and mumbles, "Go fuck yourself."

I should just keep quiet, but I don't. Not like she's going to throw my ass onto the street. She'd feel too guilty. "No thanks. I have people who do it for me. Kind of like you used to. You taught me well."

Then I'm out.

"You're late," says Jasmine when I get to Tony's Pies. She's been in a pissy mood lately.

"I always make up for it. I can deliver more pies in an hour than most people here can in two."

"Whatever." That's all she has, because she knows I'm right.

"What's your deal, anyway? It's like you've been on the rag since September." I pick up the boxes waiting for me. They're still hot. Obviously, me being a little late didn't mess anything up. Jasmine is so full of shit.

"Like you'd even know," she says.

"Know what?"

She throws up her hands. "If I'm 'on the rag' or not. You haven't been down there since before your summer vacay."

This. I should have expected it. "I've been working."

"Duh. So have I. I'm the one who got you this stupid job."

And when I said yes, fucking Jasmine was going to be one of the perks. But then summer happened.

She's staring at me. "What gives? You settle down or

something?" She can't even finish that last question, she's laughing so hard.

"You talk too much. Let me get out of here before the pizzas get cold."

"Alex!"

I wave to her as I walk to the door. "If someone calls, tell them I'm on my way."

Katie

The halls clear quickly. I noticed it more right afterwards. This Katie hasn't been paying attention, too caught up gathering her books, thinking of Alex.

"It's been a long time," says Chris, and I jump. When did he get here?

"Not long enough." Books, focusing on my books. Just get them and go go go.

He crouches down beside me. "Here, let me help you with those." He puts my books in my backpack. His fingers squeeze my knee, and I'm a pathetic, useless sculpture again.

"Shit," says a voice behind me. The cinnamon stench makes me jump. "You're starting without me?"

I grab my backpack, and Chris grabs my wrist. "Going already? Not even a thank you for the books?"

I try to get free, but he holds tighter. Ethan grabs my other wrist. "We had a deal," I say stupidly to Chris.

"I've come back to cash in."

"No," I say, trying the word out.

Ethan and Chris laugh. "Maybe if you said that the first time," says Ethan, "we'd still be together."

Chris lets go of my wrist. He motions for Ethan to do the same. But they stay close. "Look, man," says Chris. "She's saying no. We shouldn't make her do anything she doesn't want to do."

Ethan rubs his chin like he's thinking it over. "You're right. Sorry, Katie. We'll see you around."

Can it be that easy?

"Unless," says Chris, "she changes her mind."

I shake my head no. Why would I change my mind?

"Yeah," says Ethan, ignoring me. "Then, it would be okay."

They planned this. Just like before. I shake. "What is it?" I ask.

Chris raises his eyebrows. He looks at Ethan.

"Well," says Ethan, and Chris takes out his cell phone. "We have this video."

And it's me. And it's them. And I'm not saying no. And Ethan is on top of me. Then Chris. And my hands are on them, doing what they want. Why don't I remember that? He keeps playing it. When it ends, he starts it again.

I'm cold. I run to the garbage can and throw up.

"She better brush her teeth," I hear Ethan say.

"So, what's it going to be, Katie?" asks Chris. "You can come back to my house. The three of us can have some fun, and then this video is gone."

"Or," says Ethan, "you can say no, and we'll totally respect that. But who knows where the video may wind up."

"The choice is yours," says Chris.

I don't have a choice. I think of Alex, the stars. He can't see the tape.

But does everyone already know? What about what Derek said? What Marissa keeps writing in the bathrooms, not bothering to hide the marker when I see her? The looks she gives me. "You haven't told anyone?"

They look surprised, like that's not something they expected I'd ask next. "You don't exactly brag about your girlfriend cheating on you," Ethan says.

"But Marissa—"

Ethan rolls his eyes. "She's just likes making shit up. She doesn't like you for some reason. Did you know that?" He laughs and makes the sound of cats fighting.

Chris slams my locker shut. "So back to the tape. No one knows. You say yes, it stays that way. You say no, and... " He shrugs.

There can't be an and.

"I get to erase it myself," I say.

"Obviously," says Chris, bored.

I pick up my backpack, and the three of us walk out of the school.

Kyle

Each time you pick up the phone to call Julie, it starts. The quickening heartbeat, the racing pulse, the sweat. You've called her over a dozen times, and it doesn't get any better. But you like it. Crave it. Wait for it, because it's something you depend on now. You don't know what to call it, but you know it's not love or the high you felt with Sarah. But it relaxes you in a way only your mother's tranquilizers were able to do. And when it comes, you feel safe.

Tonight, she's supposed to call you, and you lie on your bed and wait. The waiting is always the hardest. Your clothes get damper, breath gets shallower. Each minute you wait, you replay the last conversation you had. What if it was the last one? What if tonight is the night she stops calling? You don't know why you want her words so much. Why her touch, that seems to come through the phone on her breath, doesn't scare you anymore. You made up your mind last night, as you drifted off to sleep, thinking about tonight, that you need her touch and more than through her voice.

When the guys at school talk about sucking this and

fucking that, you can listen without freaking. You can laugh with them and not wonder if they'll ask you to tag along to a make-out party or try to hook you up with a girl that's "so into you." They know you're taken. They know to back off. You've even been going out more because the pressure is gone. Even Alex is letting you be and not bringing home his string of hos.

But there's a part of you that's pretty sure you'll never love her. That feels guilty because you think she might. That hears it in phone pauses when you say good-bye. You hear her waiting, wondering if tonight is the night you'll add the "love you." Then, there's a tiny sigh and a catch in her voice and she says, "Yeah ... bye." You know why the catch is there. But she doesn't understand how you feel. She's survival, she's air, she's food.

And isn't that greater than love?

Katie

The cheerleaders all dress up as zombie cheerleaders for Halloween. Dark eyeliner, ripped fishnets, white makeup on our faces.

I like dress-up, but I don't think being a zombie is a stretch for me. I walk the halls dazed, waiting for Ethan or Chris to resurface with some new game. Then I remind myself it's over. Two weeks ago, in Chris's room, when they were done with me, I held the phone in my shaking hands and pressed *delete*. I scrolled through the contents over and over, making sure there were no copies. It was done. I should feel free.

"Over here, Pyramid Girl," calls Leah from the cheerleader table. I smile big as I make my way over, ignoring the too-loud swish of my cheerleading skirt. Was it always this loud? The girls at the table bend heads and whisper and giggle, and I keep smiling while hoping their whispers are not about me. They're not, I tell myself. I'm still Pyramid Girl. Invincible. No one knows.

I sit down, and fit right in with the other zombies. Ethan

is dressed as a zombie football player. He tries to feed Marissa a fry, but she pushes it away. Instead, she picks at her chicken pot pie. The only reason anyone buys the chicken pot pie is because four bites has been proven to send you rushing to the toilet with heaves. Why does Marissa want to lose more weight?

"So get this," says Trina. "You'll never believe what I heard about Mr. Stevens."

Out of the corner of my eye, I see Marissa tense and raise a spoonful of congealed chicken to her lips.

Trina leans further in. "Someone caught him and that secretary with the purple highlights doing it in the woods behind the school. You know—the pot fields?"

"Classic!" says Ethan, clapping.

"Shut up! You're not serious!" says Marissa, laying on the disbelief too thick. I see her hand shaking as she picks up another bite of chicken. "I always knew that woman was a skank."

There was a new slur in the bathroom yesterday. *Katie Taylor is a skank.* It was dark and I drew a big willow tree over it. All the leaves made my pen run out of ink. Marissa mixes the crust into the creamy mess. Does she want to be Pyramid Girl this badly? I'd give it to her, but then I won't be unbeatable anymore. I won't be able to pocket extra glitter just in case I need more magic.

"Totally," comes a chorus. "Who does that?"

Skank. Whore. Bitch. The words keep coming.

I look at Ethan, and he mouths *you.* No one else sees him.

Marissa eats another spoon of pie. One more to go. I hate her.

"Her?" I say. "Really?" Marissa looks up. They all look

up. My voice has a razor's edge. They're not used to that. "What about *him*? Why does he get off free and clear? Guys like that, you know they just use women, right? Then"— and now I look straight at Marissa—"when they've gotten everything they want, they toss her away, like the skank they know she is."

Marissa turns pale. Ethan gives me a warning look. He doesn't know why what I said upset Marissa, but he knows I upset her. He doesn't like that. She plunges her spoon deep into the pie and inhales the creamy mess. Spoon four. She gags and rushes for the bathroom. Too late. Chunks of the barely digested chicken, peas, and carrots fly to floor, just missing the garbage. She heaves again and the cafeteria erupts in "eww, gross." The bell rings, and the cheerleaders pick up their trays in unison and walk around the vomit and a crying Marissa. "Sorry, girl," says one, and keeps on walking.

Ethan's eyes are lasers. I pretend they don't scare me. He stays behind and helps clean up her barf. He never stayed behind to clean up mine.

I walk away quickly, and my phone vibrates. I know I shouldn't look. I tell myself it's Alex, even though that would be too perfect. Nothing is perfect here. It vibrates again, telling me to check my text. I look back at Marissa and Ethan, and he mouths *phone*. I open it, and he smirks. WHORE.

Alex

I'm getting ready to call Katie when I get a text from Jasmine: U need to come in.

I text back: Don't work tonight, babe. Sorry.

It's an emergency, she writes.

It's fucking pizza, I write.

Pleeease :-(she says.

Fine. Give me 20. U owe me big.

I can give you something big ... ;-)

I don't text back. She doesn't do it for me anymore. None of them do. I wake up thinking of Katie. I deliver shitty pizzas and think about what I can buy Katie with the tips. Old hos brush up against me, and I only get hard out of reflex. I haven't called Katie my girlfriend, but what else can she be?

I get to Tony's, and it's just Jasmine there, her braless tits almost hanging out of her V-neck. Fuck me. "What's the emergency?" As if I don't know.

She comes up to me and backs me into the door. Her boobs are practically in my mouth. "I'm making it up to you." She moves her skanky hand to my zipper and pulls down.

Then her mouth is on mine and her hand is doing its thing. God. I picture Katie, and Jasmine could never be her. Not with that filthy mouth. I push her away. She doesn't move. Just says, "Sshh" and keeps going. I push her harder and she rubs me harder. Goddamn.

I only want Katie to make my head—both of them—explode. How did I get this way? Fuck me if I know. "Get the hell off me, you slut!"

She stops. And pushes me hard. "Who the fuck do you think you are?" She raises her hand to slap me but I grab her wrist.

"Just relax, okay? We had fun, and it's done."

She sputters. "You're an asshole, you know that?"

I laugh. "I've been called worse."

"Get out."

"So there's no emergency?"

"Get. Out." She throws a chair at me.

"Be careful with that hand. You'll need it to make some other guy happy."

"You know," she says, voice full of desperation as I walk to the door, "when your little whore stops doing it for you— and she will—you'll come crawling back. Ask me if I'll be here waiting."

"I'll see you around, Jas. Get some rest." I make a mental note to work any shift but hers from now on.

I'm smiling as I walk to my car. I check my phone to see if Katie texted. She didn't. And an unfamiliar feeling starts in my gut. Disappointment? Over a chick? It's like she owns me.

This should scare the shit out of me, but it doesn't. Hell, I *want* her to own me.

I don't wait until I get home. I text her and tell her she needs to come to Philly. She doesn't answer right away, probably analyzing the whole thing from every angle like girls do, and I almost text her to forget it, no big deal. But then she texts: YES! Like that, all caps. Freaking exclamation point too. I text her to bring Julie. I think little bro would like that. She texts back a heart. I get in the car and tell her I'll call her as soon as I get home.

I gun the gas, go through a red light, and lucky for me the coppers are off eating donuts. At home I dial Katie's number, and realize I'm whipped as shit and damned pleased about it.

Julie

Kyle meets us outside his and Alex's townhouse. He's hopping from one foot to the other, blowing on his hands and then rubbing them together. I smile at this and at him, and put my hand up in a half-wave. Like one of those hello gestures Pilgrims and Indians supposedly gave one another. It feels dumb right after I do it, and I put my hand down quickly, but Kyle smiles. Then I forget all about how I planned to keep it cool and run across the street, my bulging duffel bag dragging on the road.

I throw my arms around his neck, and it takes him two seconds to hug me back. Two seconds too long, but I guess he's not used to girls running into his arms. Or seeing me as the running-into-guys'-arms type. I'm not used to that either. So I pull back first, since I've already shown too much. And, it's here that I get Katie a bit. Her games from the summers. Her Jersey Katie vs. Catskills Katya. Maybe you can't always let it all hang out.

"Let's bring this in," says Kyle, taking my duffel and resting his hand on my shoulder.

"Sounds good," I say and glance back to see Katie and Alex wrapped around each other, hip to hip, mouth to mouth, like they can't get close enough.

"Drink?" asks Kyle when we're inside.

"Hit me," I say, automatically feeling stupid, but Kyle laughs and gently punches me in the arm.

I relax. So Kyle and I are not the air-hogging type. We're the Spit-playing, soft-punching, joking type, and that's cool.

"Diet cola all right? Mom's on a health binge this week. Too bad you didn't come last weekend. We had mad chocolate here. She read it made you smarter. Or sexier. Or some crap."

I sip the cola and make a face. I can drink diet at home. "Maybe there's a secret stash."

He shakes his head sadly. "She's pretty committed to each hare-brained scheme she gets."

"She around?"

"Nope. Working late." He puts air quotes around the working, whatever that means.

I take another sip and hear Katie and Alex come in through the garage. Alex's bedroom is down there. I wonder if Kyle will take me on a tour. Show me his bedroom in that grand, sweeping way like it's the roped-off part of a museum. Show me the bed. We'd bounce, laugh, I'd throw a pillow and soon my arms would be pinned behind my head. I've been imagining this scenario since the summer. Chloe and I went over the details. "You have lots of lost time to make up for," she said when she found out we'd only kissed this summer. I told Chloe it was fine. I didn't need more. But I did. I do. I want the breathless kiss.

Kyle cocks his head and smiles like he's trying to figure me out. Then he takes my hand and says, "Tour?"

My heart thumps, but I play it cool. "Sure. Show me your abode." And then I want to kick myself because who talks like that, and why am I the only person on the planet who uses words on the vocab list in real life?

Of course, Kyle laughs. We're a match made in geekdom. Or my half is, anyway.

He shows me the bathroom—fluffy purple carpets, purple walls, makeup mirror with Hollywood lights around it that glow a light lavender when turned on, fuzzy purple toilet seat cover. "She always wanted daughters, and we never cared enough to redecorate. Once, though, Alex drank himself sick and purposely puked all over the seat cover. He bought her a white cover as an apology. She cleaned the purple one and put it back." He shrugs.

"Interesting."

"I know. Moving on."

There's an office, which I guess his mom worked in once a upon a time, and a guest room decorated in tans and browns, something out of a catalogue for sure. Then we get to Kyle's bedroom. I don't know what I expected. Some posters? Trophies that reveal a Kyle I don't know? But it's . . . plain. The walls are white, the bedspread navy with no patterns at all. There's a desk in the corner with open math and history textbooks, a notebook, a calculator, protractor, and a planner. The Berber carpet is my favorite part. Makes me think he and I have something else in common even though I'm sure he didn't choose it. There's a TV in the center of the room, with video games underneath it. Old video games—the joystick kind, some with the fancier controllers with the up/down keys like I've seen in gaming stores. No Wii or anything close to that. That has to mean something.

"Old school," I say, nodding at the Nintendo Mario Bros. cartridges. Right next to it is an Atari base that—no joke— has to be an antique.

He blushes. "They were my dad's. If I want to play anything current, I just go to Alex's room."

I move to his bed and plop down. Surprisingly, it bounces. I would have pegged the mattress to be really firm or saggy, not bouncy. "Nice."

He's still by the video games. I bounce on the bed again to give myself something to do, to maybe make it look fun so he'll come over. He doesn't.

"Wanna play?" I ask, getting off the bed and sitting beside the games.

This makes him happy. I finally hear movement downstairs in the kitchen. No question what Alex and Katie were doing this whole time. Kyle puts pillows behind us so we can lean back. Our shoulders touch. Our knees touch. And we play.

Katie

South Street in Philly is crazy. Alive. Lit up in the dark. So many sounds, and it's like the electricity from the street lights and store signs has entered everyone who walks on the ground. Cherry Hill has nothing like this. The noisiest, most happening place we have is the Cherry Hill Mall, and the sounds there are just incoherent noise, not living energy. *This* is what would make my mother breathe. I wonder if she was ever here. If she was, I don't know how she was able to leave. I don't know how we've lived in Cherry Hill all these years, and the only time I visited Philly was on an elementary school trip to see the Liberty Bell. It was cracked.

That time, it was just museum and back on the bus. *Your father doesn't like the city.* I remember Mother saying that now. I can see that—for him, anyway. My dad is all about the peace and quiet. Maybe that's why he chose Cherry Hill—a place where trees actually blossoming with real cherries would have been too much action. Or maybe he'd only visited the Liberty Bell too, and never set foot on South Street. Maybe he just doesn't miss what he doesn't know.

"This is *amazing*," I say to Alex. "How are you not here all the time?"

Alex shrugs. "I guess it's a little too indie for me."

"Not for me!" I yell, taking his hand. I pull it so we can run through the crowds. He laughs as we bump into people. They're all too absorbed in their own chats and cell phone worlds to give us dirty looks. They don't even notice us. It's a rush not to be noticed. To be crazy, wild, goofy and not worry someone will text about it or graffiti the bathroom walls. To not walk around and wonder if anyone here knows anything about the old Katie.

He pulls me to him and kisses me deep in the middle of the street. People walk around us like we're a permanent fixture. The kiss is a surge of power in the already blazing street. When we pull apart, I'm on fire in spite of the cold.

"I should have invited you here sooner," Alex says.

"Well, now that I've been here, I'm never leaving." I almost bite the words back, but he grins.

"Sounds good to me."

There are so many stores, and it's past nine but they're all open. Which makes sense, because if you lived here, why would you want to sleep? My stomach growls and I want to ignore it because it would mean sitting down, and all I want to do is bounce, but Alex is already pulling me toward a pizza place called Lorenzo's.

We don't go in right away, and he steps back as I take it in. Rows of muraled storefronts. The pizzeria is sandwiched between a building with a blue and red painted facade. I imagine that the people living in that apartment are super artsy types, the types who have Picasso-inspired paintings on their walls. The drawing above the pizza place, though, is even more jaw-dropping. It's a life-size painting of a chef flipping dough, rolling pin on the table.

"You have stuff like this in Cherry Hill?" asks Alex.

I laugh. "Not even close. We have a wicked mall, though."

"The pizza here is big as hell. Bet it's the best you ever had, too."

I feign shock. "Not where you work? Isn't coming here like treason or something?"

He rubs his chin in thought. "You may be right. Better not tell them." He winks, leading me inside.

There are more murals in the restaurant. Layers of an American flag over a skyline, painted lights, hearts, bubbly shapes of seats. There are no actual seats, and we stand by the counter. It has one of those mirrors that seems to go on for infinity when you look in it. Row after row of my face and Alex's. My legs are a little tired, but the pizza is good. Crisp, thin. Not the overly doughy kind the pizza places at home have.

We're only alone for a few minutes before it's packed with other guys and girls hanging all over each other. Laughing and smiling and talking too loudly. At Cherry Hill, this scene would make me tense. I'd look around for faces I knew, stiffen at anyone who rubbed too close against me, but I'm relaxed here. I slide to the floor and sit cross-legged, finishing my slice. Alex wasn't kidding about how big it was. I try to eat it neatly but give up.

"Good eats, right?" says Alex. He's already finished his two slices.

"Uh huh." It's been a good night, and now that we've had time to rest, I realize how tired I am. I could sit here for a while longer.

"Fuck," Alex suddenly mumbles under his breath.

I glance at him to see what upset him, but I can't tell. "What is it?"

"Nothing. Let's just go." He pulls me up quickly and pushes me toward the door. But he's not looking forward, just back. I look back too to make out who spooked him. There are so many kids it's hard to tell.

Outside, the cold whips at my face, and it's harder to get sucked into the noise and lights. Alex keeps looking back as he walks. "What happened in there?" I touch his arm but he's walking so fast, my arm falls away.

"Just saw some people I could do without. No big, okay?"

I nod. "Okay." I know what it's like to be surrounded by people you don't want to see.

He finally stops after we've walked some blocks. He takes my hands and turns me to him, then touches my cheek with his hand. "I'm sorry about that. You don't need to be dragged into my mess."

I want to laugh. *Me* dragged into *his* mess? He has no idea. "All I care about is being here with you." I wrap my arms around his neck and kiss him on the lips. I try to transfer warmth and safety because that's what I know I would need.

"You're amazing," he says when we've pulled away. My teeth chatter and I put my mittened hands in my pockets.

"You looked so comfortable eating pizza. How about we get you a seat?"

The world is spinning colors and voices fly in all directions, but all I want is to rest beside him. "Lead the way."

Alex

It was going great. Just me and Katie and her getting all gaga over South Street. Don't know the last time I really walked around and looked at everything. And I'm sure when I did, I didn't look at shit the way she does.

So we're just chillaxing at Lorenzo's when Jasmine walks in with her posse. I fucking swear that bitch is stalking me. Since her almost raping me at Tony's two weeks ago, she's fucking everywhere. She needs to get it through her head that I don't go after used-up trash.

I know she saw me, too. Those black eyes zeroed in on Katie like she was a bull's-eye. Fuck if I'm dealing with that shit tonight. So now we're at Cosi, doing the clichéd date s'mores thing. But for me, it's not typical. I've done lots of the fucking thing, but not so much the holding hands lovey dovey thing. Katie takes her hair out of her ponytail and puts the elastic on her wrist. Even that drives me crazy. Then she dips her finger into the chocolate and brings it to my lips. I lick it down. Shit. How does she make me want her this bad?

"Good choice," she says, taking my hand and sucking

on my finger. Her mouth does all the stuff I'd seen it do before and it's just as hot on my finger. "You like that?" Her voice is throaty. "There's more where that came from." She spears a marshmallow, dips it in the chocolate and takes little bites around, teasing me. Like she doesn't know she's driving me crazy.

She feeds me a chocolate-dipped marshmallow and sips her hot chocolate. I wonder if Mom will show tonight. Not that it changes anything. She's never cared about the chicks I brought home before. She basically ignored all of them or just yelled about them eating our food. With Jasmine, it was the perfume. Mom claimed she knew when she was in the house because it smelled like roses—the "cheap-ass" kind. I don't know cheap from expensive, but the smell gave me headaches. Still does.

Katie has stopped trying to be sexy and is inhaling the marshmallows. I lean back in my chair and close my eyes. It's good to feel chill.

But then there's a voice at my ear. "He-ey," she says. "Haven't seen you around, yo." My eyes snap open and the rose stink hits my nose.

Kyle

It's late, and the house is still empty. The wind howls outside and Julie moves closer to you. "My thumbs are getting tired," she says, pausing her game and putting her hand on your thigh. She lifts her chin at you, throwing you another hint that she wants to be kissed. You want to—have wanted to all night—and don't know why you haven't.

You thought about it while talking on the phone, all the nights before this one. You imagined it when you found out she would be coming to see you. Remembered her summer lips on yours. All these hours, while you were playing Ms. Pac Man and your knee rubbed on hers, you wanted to stop the game—even though Ms. Pac Man hadn't eaten all the cherries yet—and push Julie down and tug at her hair. So what stopped you?

Your days have been filled with quiet and routine for months now. Sometimes Alex visited your room—always knocking first—and gave you a noogie and played video games. Like you were both always normal. Like there was never anything shady between you. Sometimes you even told him a little about Julie, and he made an inappropriate comment or two but nothing demented.

But you're still haunted by the past. Still afraid that he might barge into your room at any moment, friend-with-benefits in tow, and tell you to stop being a pussy. That he can appear while you and Julie are entangled and squash anything that's there. Change it all once again.

Tonight, though, you know Katie will keep him busy. Then they'll come home and retreat downstairs, not seeing you again until the morning. So you have time. Hours. Your pulse slows. You find yourself breathing easier.

"I'm tired," she says, getting off the floor. She grabs her duffel and goes to the bathroom. When she comes back, she's wearing a green tank top and owl-printed pajama pants. You smile at her and she blushes.

"They're dumb, aren't they?" she asks.

"No," you say. They're sweet, young. So very Julie.

She starts walking to your bed, then stops and turns around.

"It's your room. You should have the bed." Her voice is defeated, like she's not even going to suggest you share a bed.

You're mad at yourself. Why do you have to be such a wuss? She's not asking to have sex, for Christ's sake, just share a bed. When the two of you were kids, you used to lie side by side on the pullout at the lake house and play cards. "You're not sleeping on the floor," you tell her, and watch as she hesitantly lies down on the bed. "Can I lie with you?"

Her eyes go wide, and she moves closer to the side so you have enough room. You use the remote to turn off the lights and turn on the TV. Some comedy shows that get you both laughing, that make the fact you're spooning her less scary.

You both start to fall asleep, and you let the screen go dark. She moves around to get more comfortable and faces you. You stroke her hair and pull her close to you. You put your mouth on hers and she kisses you back, like you're what she's been needing. Like you're her food, her drink, her air, too. And you don't let yourself think at all. Just move your hands and legs and pull and tug at clothes, under clothes. Your breath quickens. Hers does too.

"Kyle," she whispers, and her voice brings you back to the moment, the room. She moves to take her shirt off, but you stop her. You want to look at her as she is, silly owl pajamas and all. You don't need more. You're not Alex. You wrap your arms around her and hold her, using your fingers to brush the hair from her eyes; then you close yours. For the first time in a long time, you fall asleep at peace.

Katie

H e-ey," she says to Alex, her sparkly earrings dangling by her chin. "Haven't seen you around, yo." Her hair is dark and wavy and her eyes black. She smells like roses. I smile at her, playing nice even though it seems they may have had a thing. Even though I feel Barbie-plain beside her. She sneers at me and taps her studded nails on the table. I shiver.

"Where've you been hiding yourself?" She leans in too close to Alex. She's wearing a red, fuzzy sweater with a deep V-neck, and I can see the red lacy push-up peeking out.

She leans closer to me and I can smell alcohol on her breath. Just smelling it makes me nauseated. "I'm Jasmine," she slurs, dipping her finger into the melted chocolate and then putting it by Alex's mouth. He pushes it away, and she shrugs. "More for me."

"I'm Katie." Because I have to say something. Alex's face is red. He clenches his fist. He looks like he'd hit Jasmine if we weren't somewhere public.

"Kaaatie," says Jasmine, laughing. "Such a...wholesome...name."

Alex bangs the table and pushes his chair back. "Let's go."

"So soon?" she smirks, trying to grab his wrist. "Katie and I didn't even have a chance to chat."

"Go fuck yourself, because you know there's no way in hell I'm doing it for you."

This shuts her up, and she switches from sultry to weepy. "Because you have Barbie, is that it?"

She keeps shouting as we walk to the door, and I expect her to call me a slut, a whore, to reveal everything Alex doesn't know.

He sticks his middle finger up at her and keeps walking, so she calls my name instead. I keep moving, too, but can't tune her out. "You think you're hot shit, Kaaatie? I bet you're a perfect cheerleader. You just wait. One day he'll dump your lily-white ass, too."

Outside, Alex punches the brick building and yells "Fuck!" I let him and stay behind. I watch Jasmine through Cosi's window. She's still at the table, her head in her hands, her shoulders heaving. She pushes the chocolate away and the pot falls to the floor. She slams her fist on the table, just like Alex did.

He finally comes to me, but he's still breathing heavy. His fists are still clenched.

"I should have never let her talk to you," he says.

"It's fine. It's done. Let's go home, okay?"

I wrap my arm around his waist and he does the same. I don't ask him any questions, and he doesn't give any information. I wonder what happened between them. His eyes were mean, not like I've ever seen them. Why does he hate her? Were there other Jasmines?

We stop by his townhouse. "I don't want you worrying about her," he says, as if reading my mind.

I nod. I never want his eyes to look at me that way.

He tilts my chin up. "You're my Katie. You're special."

You're my Pyramid Girl.

For a second I wonder if she was special, too. "And Jasmine—"

"Is a dumb whore and nothing like you."

Julie

Winter break is here and it couldn't have happened soon enough. Chloe almost died when I told her about making out with Kyle last month. And now that I know what that was like, I need more. Licking my lips, closing my eyes, and pretending it's him (not a pillow) I'm kissing has gotten old. Mama said he and Alex can come here, and I've been counting down for weeks. I'll be spending New Year's Eve with a boy! *Kissing* a boy when that ball drops. Talk about romance. Chloe says I need to tell her everything.

Mama doesn't ask for the same. She didn't ask about my weekend in Philly. Didn't ask if I'd been kissed. I think she thinks it's all in my head. I mean, she knows Kyle is a boy of real flesh, but I doubt she believes his skin has ever touched mine. Or will. That's the real reason she said Kyle could come. I think a part of her wants to see if he's real or if her poor, ugly daughter made him up.

It shouldn't matter.

Daddy believes me. Too much, in fact. Right now, he's trying to talk Mama out of the two of them leaving the house for the night. "They're teenage girls home alone with teenage boys!" he keeps repeating, putting inflection on new words each time like saying it louder or differently will change Mama's mind.

She sighs and says, "Katie knows to play it smart. Right, Katie? You know to be a good girl."

When she says this, Katie squirms and looks away, but says, "Yes, mom. I'll be good."

I want to laugh, because Katie and Alex have not been "good." But it's like she and Mama have their own code and are talking about something more than sex. It's totally beyond me.

Daddy's face gets red. "What about Julie? She's still young and impressionable."

That's right, I think. What *about* me?

Mama laughs. "Kyle isn't the type. And this is our Julie." She walks over, strokes my hair. As always, my head moves to her for approval, like I'm a marionette, and her voice pulls the strings. "We don't have to worry about any of that with her."

It could be taken as *because she knows better* or *she's brainier,* but I know Mama too well. There's no reason to worry about those things with Julie because she's more Skipper than Barbie.

Daddy sighs and shakes his head. I know *he* knows better. So it shouldn't matter what Mama thinks.

It shouldn't matter that I overhead her yesterday, asking Katie if Kyle actually saw me as something more than a friend. What should matter is Daddy getting more annoyed with Mama over her disbelief that I could possibly have a boyfriend. What should matter is only caring about what Kyle thinks. What should matter is what is important to Kyle and *me*, not to Mama or to Chloe or to the other girls at my lunch table.

But that's not how it goes. Part of me is all about Kyle, all about Kyle and me, all about the little hearts I draw with our initials. The other part is about how we look to everyone else.

Katie

I'm learning we all play games.

Marissa's clothes hang more. She doesn't come to lunch much anymore. When she does, she spends it holding Ethan's hand like she'd float away without him. Sometimes he comes to lunch without her, the days she forgets to tell him she's somewhere else. With someone else ... she stopped confiding in me last spring, but I think she and Mr. Stevens are still going strong. She can't have it both ways. She can't have two guys and two lives.

These days, when I crave Alex's touch, when I cross off days on my calendar, each X bringing me closer to him, I wonder how I used to last from one summer to the next. How it was so easy to leave him, the creek, the swings behind. It's funny I was so confident. So sure I could have both, swinging my pom-poms and playing popular when the heat passed. What's more amazing is that it worked at all. That it would have still worked had it not been for the night I was pulled under in my haze of beer and bubblegum shots and blue punch. Where was my mother then? *Don't mix beer and liquor,*

Katie. That was my downfall is what she should have told me when I still played with Barbies. *See how Barbie reclines with her mixed cocktail with the little umbrella? It's all about control, honey.* But I found all this out too late.

Today, the lunch table—complete with Ethan and Marissa—is filled with talk of winter vacation and New Year's Eve parties.

"Your man is coming to visit, right?" asks Trina. "Girls, you have to see him. Mmm. Mmm." She thinks she's helping, but I wasn't thrilled when Mama said Alex should come to Cherry Hill. I really don't want him in this world. "C'mon," says Trina. "Show them a pic."

I take out my cell phone and show them my Alex shots. Alex by the lake. Alex with his hand out like he's saying "no photos, please." Alex and me close up, his arm around my shoulders, pulling me to him.

"Da-amn," says Leah. "I wouldn't mind sharing." She winks at me like she's kidding.

I laugh. "Nah, he's all mine."

Ethan grabs the cell and my heart jumps. He starts pressing keys. Is he texting him? I lunge toward him and grab the phone out of his hand. My nail scratches his skin. The table goes silent.

"What the fuck, bitch?" His eyes stare into mine, like he's threatening me to break contact. That afternoon of him, and Chris, and me, he made me stare into his eyes the whole time. I look away.

"Yeah, I thought so," he mumbles. "Let's go, Mariss."

She's a zombie again, and he has to pull her out of the

chair. I don't think she even knows what just went down. She holds tightly to his arm. He's her anchor to this world, the one keeping people from getting suspicious, the one who lets her play her game of two Marissas. But she's fading. It's a matter of time until she cracks. I watch them leave the cafeteria, and Ethan gently moves her hand to another part of his arm. I want to tell her it's just easier to pick. That she can't have it all. But who am I to say?

My cell vibrates with a message. My eyes flash to Ethan, but he and Marissa are gone. I exhale and open the phone.

It's from Alex: Hi, Sexy.

Hi, hot stuff, I text back.

The bell rings and my table picks up their trays full of half-eaten food and throws them in the trash. We wave our fingernails, painted in our school colors, in the air and do an exaggerated cheerleader wave—jazz-hands style.

"Don't forget New Year's Eve, Katie," says Trina.

"I want to meet that hottie of yours," says Leah, her voice coated with saccharine. "Okay, girls, later! Air kisses! Mmmwah!"

"Mmmwah!" I shout back, words covered with my own artificial sweetener. I blow them both kisses and giggle down the hall. I clutch my cell with Alex's message because that's what grounds me. That reminds me what's truly real.

Alex

We pull into Katie and Julie's driveway, and their dad is the first one I see.

He stares at Kyle and me like he's sizing us up. "Boys," he says, nodding. "Good to see you both again." Then he sticks out his hand. That thing's got muscle. Who would have thunk it, with that paunch? I guess there has to be something besides the gut to keep Anna around.

Kyle puts his hand out first. He's good like that. "You too, Sir." Sir! Poser.

I wait a second too long, and Mr. T eyes me harder and puts his hand down. "Julie is inside," he says to Kyle.

"Thank you," says Kyle, all polite and shit, and lugs his duffel bag up the porch.

I move to go too, and Mr. T puts his arm on my shoulder. "I care about Katie, okay?"

Well, fuck, I care about her too. What kind of asshole does he think I am? I tense and want to rip his arm off. "I care about her, too."

"She's … she's … " He pauses and takes his hand off my

shoulder. Spit it out, old man! "Look, she seems like she has no worries or problems, and I don't know if that's true or not. But don't give her any shit, okay? Sometimes she looks breakable. Don't break her. Got it?"

What the hell? I don't even know where to go with this. I want to tell him I waited to have sex with her. I could have taken her that night she was trashed, but I didn't. She's different. "I got it," I say, and head up to the house with my duffel bag. Anna honks the horn and yells at him to get in the car, but I still feel Papa's eyes on my back. I don't turn around.

Katie ambushes me at the door, throwing her skinny arms around my neck. "What took you so long?" I hear the car peel away.

"Your dad and I were having a heart-to-heart."

She laughs like she doesn't believe me. "Whatever. Just glad you're here."

"Yeah, me too, baby." I squeeze her back and feel her bones through her thin sweater. How come I never noticed before? I lighten my grip. What if she really could break that easily?

Speaking of breaking, I need out. Where are Anna's fuck-me eyes when I need them? I'll take them over Daddy Dearest's warden impersonation any day. "Ready to jet? I hear you have mad cool malls in Jersey."

Katie

"You weren't kidding about the mall," says Alex. "Not bad."
I shrug. "It's fine, but they're changing things here everyday. Can't depend on any store staying."

"Sweet!" he says, dragging me to Radio Shack. I follow
him around and look at gadgets I don't understand while he
waxes poetic on the many ways to use a cell phone and how
easy it is to record things these days. As if I didn't know.

When I see him losing steam, I lure him to the exit with
kisses. "My turn," I say pulling him into the Disney Store.
An employee dressed as Prince Charming carries in an arm-
ful of princess dresses and hangs them on a rack beside me.
When I was little, my mother bought me every princess dress
made. She has photos of me in Cinderella slippers, dress,
and crown; Snow White blue ribbon, puffy dress, and shoes;
Sleeping Beauty, Little Mermaid, all of them. When they
came out with a new style, she bought me that one, too. I
loved it. I *was* that girl. The one who'd tell people she'd be
a princess when she grew up. Not Julie. Julie wanted to be a

doctor. A police woman. When she was in fifth grade, it was a foreign ambassador.

I pick up one of the dresses now. It's lavender and that shiny, crinkly material. They must make them in larger sizes now—for the girls who have never given up on the princess dream—because it goes down to my ankles. "What do you think?" I ask Alex, twirling around.

He raises his eyebrows at me and licks his lips. Funny what turns guys on. "I will have to protect you with my large, princely sword."

I see Prince Charming lean in to hear more. Alex sees too and winks at me. "She only plays with my sword," he says to Charming, who turns red and scurries away.

"You're bad," I giggle, putting the dress back on the rack.

"You don't know the half of it."

"Oh yeah?" I say, pulling him behind a six-foot display of Mickey Mouse and his friends. "You been holding back?" I kiss him hard, and almost feel bad Daisy and Minnie have to witness such behavior.

"You're so hot," he murmurs against my neck. "Didn't think you were into the whole voyeur thing."

"You'd be surprised. Katie *loooves* the whole voyeur thing," says a voice behind me, and Alex and I jump apart. My skin burns.

She laughs, like she was making a joke.

"Oh, does she now?" says Alex, pulling me to him again, thinking Marissa is really just busting on me. But I'm a voice-less statue.

"You're not going to introduce me, Kate? I'm Marissa."

She extends her serpentine hand. I move my head to look at her, and there's something off about her. Her eyes dance, unfocused. Her cheeks look a little more hollow than before break.

"Alex," he says, shaking her hand.

"The pictures didn't lie," she says, moving herself too close to him. Alex tenses. He moves closer to me and puts his arm around my shoulder. I shake under his touch.

He eyes Marissa again, taking her in. "Well, Katie and I need to jet. Nice meeting you."

Marissa grips my wrist. *Chris holding my wrists tight.* "Do you really have to go? I really needed to talk to you about something. Girl stuff." She bats her eyes at Alex.

Alex holds on to my other arm, like it's a Katie tug of-war. He's stronger, but Marissa has some evil sorceress potion up her sleeve. She will find me later if I leave now. I smile at Alex. "It's all right. I'll be out in a few." Then I kiss him extra long for good measure, hoping his Charming kiss can stave off Marissa's powers.

"What's up?" I ask, when Alex leaves to sit on the bench outside the store.

She twirls her oily hair; her eyes dancing some more. She laughs. "Not much. How about you? Things going super swell?"

What does she want? I think of the voyeur comment. Could she know about that afternoon with Ethan and Chris? No, Ethan wouldn't be that stupid. Nothing good would come from him telling Marissa. What then? I bide time, try to be nice. "All's good. For you too, it seems. I can tell Ethan really likes you." I smile my big, peppy cheerleader grin.

"Lucky, lucky me." She paces.

I think of how to calm her. I think of touching her arm to steady her, but can see her baring her teeth and snapping at it. She smacks her lips as if reading my thoughts.

I glance at the bench. Alex is watching us. He looks ready to pounce himself. He must see there's something wrong with her, too.

"Nothing you want to talk to me about?" she asks, face too close to mine.

Is this about Mr. Stevens? Is she afraid I'll tell? "Like what?"

"'Like what,'" she mimics. "Look, bitch." Her voice drops to a growl. "Don't play with me. I didn't forget that you know. That was a good show in the caf the other day." Spit flies out of her mouth. "But what *you* don't know"—she giggles, like we're two friends at a sleepover—"is that I know stuff, too."

I lean on Mickey's arm. From the corner of my eye, I see Alex walking toward the store. *What does she know?* Ethan said she's just making stuff up.

"So, here's the plan. If you open your trap—if *anyone* finds out *anything*—that dreamy boy of yours will know the kind of whore you really are. Got that, *my Pyramid Girl*?" And the way she says it, it's just the way Ethan said it that night. She *has* to know. But how?

My mouth opens and closes without sound. I feel Alex at my side. "What did you say to her?" he shouts at Marissa.

"Nothing," I manage to say. "I just need to eat something."

"That would be a good idea," says Marissa, voice chock full of Sweet'N Low again. "Take care."

Alex clenches a fist. "What's with that bitch?"

But I can barely focus over images coming at me. Chris and Ethan are everywhere. The benches, the floor, the fake plants. *Tell me you like it. Say you CHOSE to be here. Have you been practicing?* Their voices are around me, in my head. Then the words: *Whore, skank, bitch.* The storefront windows are covered with them too. It all plays on repeat and there is no escape.

Julie

When the house is empty except for me and Kyle, I grab his hand.

"The parents will be gone all night," I whisper. It's funny. For all Mama's talk about the lake houses being too Russian, and never speaking Russian to me and Katie, she always celebrates New Year's Eve big—Russian style.

"That's good," says Kyle. "Your mother freaks me out. She's like a cartoon character. When she speaks, it's almost as if I can see her words as blocks of ice hanging in the air."

I open my mouth to defend her, but why? He's right.

"Let me show you my room," I say, dragging him. It's moments like these that I work hardest to ignore what Mama thinks because what teenage boy wouldn't be stoked at the idea of a night alone with his girlfriend? What guy wouldn't be running up those stairs ahead of me, stripping off his clothes as he sprinted? I guess I can't have everything—the sensitive, funny guy and also the one who wants to rip your clothes off.

In my room, I push him down on my bed and pull at

his shirt. I move my hand over his jeans. He moans. I work harder. "Julie," he says, his voice wanting. "Julie." Moans. He pulls me to him and kisses me deep and hard. His breathing is heavy as he undoes the buttons of my shirt and we both take our shirts off. He gets on top of me, and I like the feel of the rough rub of his jeans against my stomach, of his heart beating quickly against my own. Soon, his breathing and heart slow, and when I look at him, he's smiling.

He's happy. Like no-care-in-the-world happy, not his usual look that's clouded with too much thinking.

"That was," he says, breathing hard, "that was..."

"Awesome," I say.

Alex

I finish two burgers and Katie is picking at a lettuce leaf, still pale as all hell. That Marissa chick was no doubt a whack job, but Katie won't talk.

"You want me to beat her up?" I ask, trying to get her to smile.

She stares at her salad, then around the room like she's waiting for someone to ambush her. She doesn't look at me at all. I wave my hand in her face, and she finally looks up.

"You want to leave?" she says. But she makes no move to go. It's almost like she's asking if I want to leave *her*. Could that be what she's asking? What the hell did that cunt say to her?

"Talk to me. It can't be that bad," I say. She puts her face in her hands. "C'mon. Don't make me use my sword." Still no smile. Christ.

"You'll hate me," she whispers.

"No chance," I say. And I mean it, because what could she possibly say that would make me hate her?

She takes a deep breath. "Before we were, like, how we are

now ... like, back when we didn't ask each other about what happened, when you did your thing and I did mine ... " She bites her lip. I know where this is going, and I suck in air.

"You were with someone else. Fine. I get it." I don't like hearing it, but that was the plan. I was with plenty of hos, too. It was part of the rules. But it's done. "But you're not with anyone now, right?"

She shakes her head no.

"Okay, then. Moving on, right?" I take her hands, and she's still shaking.

She shakes her head no again. "Back then, back then ... " Her voice gets choked up and she stutters on the words.

"Forget it. I don't care." What the hell is she going to say?

"Just let me say this. So, there was this night. I drank too much. This girl, Leah, she's our captain ... " Like I give a fuck who she is. "Had this vodka. I did too many shots. They gave me other pretty shit to drink. I know I shouldn't have gone along with it, but it was supposed to be this big thing because I became Pyramid Girl." What the hell is Pyramid Girl? "I didn't know what was going on."

Fuck. Is this why she didn't want to drink, this past summer?

She's crying harder and hiccuping, and when she gets herself together and opens her mouth to speak, she starts all over again. People are staring at us, like I did something to her. I told her father I wouldn't break her.

Nothing could be worth this. It's not like she slept with anyone else. So she might have done some other borderline stuff. Maybe danced around naked or some shit. I can get past that. I know I can get past that, especially if she was trashed. I give her an out.

"So, you did some crap you wish you hadn't?"

She hiccups and nods.

"Because you were drunk?"

She nods again.

"And now this Marissa cunt is holding something over you?"

She's like a bobblehead doll.

I take a deep breath. "It happens. You were trashed. I don't care."

She opens her mouth, and I put my finger against it. "Sssh," I say. "It will be okay." But her eyes flash scared. "I love you. There's nothing you could have done that would change that."

The grateful look on Katie's face, the face that minutes ago thought I was going to dump her, is awesome. "We're good then?" I ask. She stares at me. "Nothing else you want to tell me, right?"

Katie

These are the things I can never tell him.

That day I went home with Chris and Ethan, I wasn't drunk. I had no excuse.

They took turns. They took their time. They told me to say I liked it. They pinched me if I wasn't wearing the Pyramid Girl smile. So I smiled. The whole time. Ethan only asked for oral (because he had a girlfriend and he wasn't a cheater). I did it. Chris touched me. They both made me tell them they were the best I ever had. My voice caught. The smile fell off. They said that's all I had to say and we'd be done. I could press *erase*. I put the smile back on and said it. They gave me the phone, and I deleted all of it. Gone, gone, gone.

Alex asks me now, eyes scared: "We're good then? Nothing else you want to tell me, right?"

I stare into his eyes. He thought I was a virgin when we did it. I didn't miss the fear in his eyes when he thought I was going to tell him too much. I remember how he looked at Jasmine.

"That's all you would really want to hear," I say, my voice still cracking.

He pulls me closer to him. Strokes my hair. Calls Marissa a whore. Tells me I'm special. Tells me everything that I want to hear. But he never says I'm wrong, that he really does want to know everything and will love me just the same.

Kyle

When you think of Julie, you waver between happiness and apprehension. When you only think of her face, her fingers in yours, her jokes, that's when it's easy. When you think of the night the two of you spent together at her house, the night that felt so good but where you couldn't sleep for hours after she had fallen asleep, where you stayed in her bed, staring at the ceiling, drenched in cold sweat, thinking it shouldn't have been so easy, trying to figure out why, even though Alex didn't make you, even though she wanted to touch you like that, you still felt scared and dirty. When you think of that night, you want to tell her maybe the two of you are making a mistake, maybe you should slow things down.

Then you think of her face the next morning, of the way she held you tight like she needed you, of how giddy and *secure* she felt, not the Julie of the green bathing suit, and you know you can't say that. Know you have to just focus on the happiness, know that you just have to get past your anxiety because it will be worth it in the end. *She* is worth it.

So today, Valentine's Day, the day you can make

everything perfect for her, you do. You go all out. You send balloons to her house. Big, red, heart-shaped ones, and six roses—one for each month you've been together. You imagine the look on Mrs. Taylor's face (the Ice Queen, you call her) when she sees that all these things are for Julie, and you know it will mean that much more. But that isn't all. You got Chloe's number off Julie's cell and told her you wanted to buy six heart-shaped lollipops the student council was selling. She was more than happy to tell you how to do that. You played the super boyfriend card and told Chloe about the surprises you were sending to Julie's house. You could hear Chloe clapping her hands over the phone. "I can't wait until Julie's bitch of a mom sees all this stuff. God, you're like the best boyfriend ever. Any more of you at home?"

"Nope. My mom decided two angels were enough." And a part of you thought she should have just stopped at the first creation.

"Well," said Chloe, "your mom must be cool to help you pay for all these things."

"Something like that." But your mother doesn't know you've been pocketing her cash instead of spending it on food. Your dinners for the last few weeks have been a slice of pizza, an order of fries, or one burrito. You asked them to throw in extra plates and napkins so you could jam the trash and make it look like you've been eating. But you don't feel bad. You figure it's the least she can do for you. She can spend years paying you back and it still won't be enough. Not enough for your father and not for what Alex became after he died.

Katie

My school is abuzz with I love you's and the sounds of kissing. I pass Ethan and Marissa, hands all over each other, at his locker. She's holding a basket of red lollipops, and when she sees me staring she gives me the middle finger, but that doesn't pause the kissing. In my head, I stick up my middle finger too.

Julie runs up to me before lunch, a bouquet of red lollipops in hand. "Can you believe Kyle?" she gushes, and I gush with her because she deserves to gush.

She looks at my empty hands. "I bet Alex sent you something at home."

I shrug. "Maybe." But in my head we're already unraveling. He hasn't talked or looked at me differently since the mall, but it's like the air has shifted. Like the thing I was afraid of most, of our worlds colliding, of the earth, the sidewalks, the grass finally exploding with all their knowledge, has started.

Julie puts on a fake pout. "Oh boy. What's with the gloom and doom, big sister? He'll come through."

"I know," I say, with my fake cheer-happy face.

Julie doesn't buy it. "Uh uh. You are not sulking." And she drags me to the lunchroom where everyone is cuddling with their boyfriends and giving me their fake sympathetic faces. Julie plops down at my table like she belongs there, and Leah makes a face.

"What's with the frosh?" she asks, sucking on her lollipop.

Julie snorts. Having a boyfriend has made her brave. "This frosh," she says pointing to herself, "doesn't want to miss what her sister's hot-as-hell boyfriend got her for Valentine's Day."

Leah rolls her eyes. "Whatever."

And it's like serendipity, because at that moment the cafeteria doors swing open and a secretary walks to our table, pizza box and heart balloons in hand. "Katie," she says, nodding like she's presenting me with the royal crown.

My lunch table stops talking. Julie bounces in her seat. I open the box and laugh. It's a heart-shaped pizza, and *I LOVE YOU* is spelled out in pepperoni, and it's dorky and so unlike Alex that I love it.

I share the pie with my table, even though only Julie deserves a slice. Even though they are fawning over the pie and telling me how lucky I am but are crazy jealous. "See?" Julie whispers. "Didn't I tell you?"

"You did," I say, taking a large bite of my slice. And it's as if the earth stopped shaking, like the crack in the surface has closed itself up again.

| Spring |

Julie

Girl," says Chloe, "I gotta pee." She's bouncing from one foot to the other. "There's no way I'm making it to the upstairs bathroom."

She sprints to the bathroom by the lunchroom—the one in the upperclassman wing where no freshperson dares to tread. I follow her because there's power in numbers, and because it's after school and the chance of running into an upperclassman is smaller.

I don't know what I expect to find there, but it's nothing exciting. Same beige tiles as upstairs, same dirty mirrors. I try the soap dispenser. Ah, there's the difference. The soap comes out on the first try without me having to whack the dispenser. The perks.

I hear the toilet flush, but Chloe doesn't come out. "Chloe?"

She doesn't answer, but I see her crouching down, then

getting up and crouching down again by the other side of the toilet. "What are you doing?"

She finally opens the door, her face disbelieving.

"What? Are the rumors true? Are there monsters in the toilets?"

"You need to see this."

"Sure, drama queen," I laugh, and then she shows me, and I stop laughing.

The walls are covered with the words. Words about Katie. There are trees, oodles of trees surrounding them, trees I recognize from Katie's doodles, but I can still make out all the names. "Fuck," I whisper.

I go to another stall, and there are more. In black marker, in pink, in blue. Everywhere.

I hear another stall open. White cheerleader shoes walk out. She sees me and smirks. "I hope you're learning something," she says.

I don't remember her name, but I know who she is. She sits at Katie's lunch table. She's below Katie on the pyramid. She's dating Ethan. Marissa. She's holding a red marker. It's uncapped, and she doesn't try to hide it. "Later, Katie's sister," she says, all confident, like she owns the world.

When she's gone, I run to the stall she was in. There's fresh red marker on the walls. More words. I grab a paper towel and put it under running water. I scrub at the fresh red but it only smudges a little. My scrubbing makes the words bigger. "Fuck!"

"Do you know why?" Chloe asks.

"How the hell would I know?" I shout at her.

"Jeez, chill. I didn't write this stuff."

I know she didn't. It was that smirky, Pyramid Girl wannabe. But why? Is being Pyramid Girl *that* amazing? And why didn't Katie tell me? How long has this been going on?

"Are you going to say anything to her?" Chloe asks.

"No. She obviously doesn't want me to know."

Chloe shrugs, but I know she's just pretending to be cool and calm. "Girls can be so two-faced. I doubt it's anything. At least no one in our grade ever uses this bathroom."

At least there's that.

Kyle

You don't like South Street. Too noisy, too busy, too mobbed. So you take Julie somewhere better. There's a marina, and it's better at night with the boats lit up, but she's not staying that long today.

You walk to the docks, fingers intertwined. It's sixty degrees out, and your clasped hands emit just the right amount of heat. A warm breeze blows her hair off her face and you stop walking and kiss her.

She smiles, but you can tell she's thinking about something else. "I don't have the power I once did," you say, a little afraid it may be true.

"No, silly. Those lips are ma-gi-cal. I'd show you just *how* magical if Dad hadn't decided to pick *now* to stand up to my mother." She pulls you to her and kisses you deep.

"And why doesn't he want you to stay over?" you say when she lets you go.

She rolls her eyes. "I think he's afraid we're all getting too close."

You can see that. At the marina, you watch boats sail and dock. Julie looks at them wistfully.

"You think those people appreciate what they have?" she asks.

You shrug. "Probably not."

"Huh." Then she's quiet again.

"So what is it? Let me be a good boyfriend."

She laughs. "You already are." Then she tells you about Katie and the bathrooms. The words set your skin on edge. They twist your stomach. They make you fear what you always had.

"You can't tell Alex," you blurt out, and she looks at you like you're crazy.

"Yeeeah," she says, really slowly like you're an idiot. "Because *that's* what I was thinking."

"Sorry. Of course you wouldn't." But the boats seem to be headed right at you and you think you're going to pass out. You feel her staring at you.

"How is this about *you?*" She's annoyed and you can't answer her.

"Sorry," you say again. You focus on the sound of the water, the ship horns, the plane overhead until you're grounded again and back on the dock.

"*Anyway*, why do you think she never told me? Never mind," she adds before you can think of something to say. "I know why. But why would anyone write that? I mean, it's not like one wall or even one stall. It's *all* walls in *all* the stalls. There's like five lines about bitchy teachers and the rest is Katie."

"Maybe she's just jealous." But you know there has to be more to it.

Julie nods. "Yeah, that's what Chloe said."

That Chloe is smart. You grab the lifeline. "Right. And didn't you say that girl is dating Katie's ex?"

Julie's face lights up. "That's it! Of course! Maybe she thinks Ethan liked Katie more. I mean, she *is* Pyramid Girl. Apparently that's a big deal."

You don't want to hear her talk anymore. You pull her to a bench and kiss her until she only speaks back in tongue. There's no one else there, and you let your hands roam over her clothes because you know this will stop all conversation. But you can't really feel her through your numbness. And after a few minutes, Julie pulls away too.

"I'm sorry," she says. "I'll make it up to you. I just can't stop thinking about it. And this is going to sound awful, but you know what I keep wondering?"

You don't want to know.

"I keep thinking, 'Does everyone know? Did everyone see those stalls?' And this is the worst part, but I wonder if that's what they think about me? Like, when they see me, do they think, 'There goes the whore's sister?'"

You close your eyes. *Stop calling her that.*

"What do you think?" she says, moving closer.

You think you're not liking her very much right now. "I think you're worried over nothing."

She sighs. "Yeah, maybe you're right. It's just that things

are better for me now. I have a boyfriend, and not just any boyfriend, but someone super cool like you. And I just don't need this. If people in my grade found out, I'd die, you know?"

"Stop worrying about it." Your voice is tense. She's being so unlike the Julie you think you know.

"Fine," she snaps.

"Fine," you say, but you don't snap. You know that's what she's waiting for, but you don't want the drama. You stare out to the water. She gives an exaggerated sigh, and you ignore it.

"My dad will be here soon," she says.

You walk back home in silence, but you know she's still thinking. With each stomp, with each kick of stone.

"You know," she says when you're almost home, "it's not like I'm a horrible person or something. Normal people think like I do."

You don't agree, so you tell her what she probably already knows. "I guess I'm not normal."

Julie

Marissa smirks at me whenever she sees me now. Today she's waiting by my locker after school. She's wearing a sleeveless turtleneck and jeans. Her hair is pulled back neatly with a blue ribbon. But when she smiles, there's lipstick all over her teeth.

"Excuse me," I say. Why is she here?

"Of course," she says, stepping aside so I can open my locker.

I get my backpack, and she's still there. "Can I help you?"

She laughs. "You and your sister sure got balls."

What could Katie have done that deserves this? Stolen her boyfriend? Seems like it's the other way around. Last year and this past summer, I would have said Katie deserved whatever was coming to her, but I can tell she's different now. We're friends. Almost.

"Stop trashing my sister," I say.

"I don't need to. She's trash all on her own."

I want to hit her, but I know she'll make my life hell. "Oh please," I say. "I'm sure you have your own skeletons."

I didn't think it was possible for her face to get any paler, but it does. Now it makes sense. Does Katie have something on *her*? Is she trying to make Katie's life hell so people won't ask about her own? I wasn't going to tell Katie, but now there's a reason. Now Marissa is in *my* face. Now I—no, we, Katie and I—can make her stop.

"You just watch your back," she says, but I can tell what I said messed her up.

"Sure thing." I know I'll now be watching hers.

Katie

Julie runs into my room, her cheeks pink with excitement. "You will not believe what Marissa did," she says.

The room spins. The chills start.

Julie doesn't notice. She talks. I hear "bathroom stalls," "your name everywhere," "who does she think she is?"

Her mouth opens and I don't hear words.

"Katie!" she yells. "I *said*, why did she do it?"

I shrug. At least I think I do. I'm too frozen to tell. "Stupid rumors," I say.

"She's not going to get away with this, right? This is what we do." She's acting like some superhero. She's going to save me. Right the wrongs. Bring justice. The best way to do this is to do nothing. She's still talking. "We figure out what she's hiding, because it's sooo obvious there's something, and then we've got her."

"No."

She looks like I slapped her. Like I thwarted her mission to save the world. "Don't you *care*?"

"It's stupid, Julie. Just let it go." My teeth chatter. The whispers start. Chris and Ethan are circling me.

"What's the matter with you? If it were me, and it kinda is because she's talking smack to *me* now, I'd want to do something."

"Well, I'm not you." Am I shouting? It's hard to hear.

She eyes me, getting angry. "God, you're such a wimp. You just want to run away from everything. It's just like with the chickens!"

I almost tell her then. But the whispers are loud, loud, loud, and I can't think. Chris and Ethan are in my face and I can't breathe. When I look up again, she's gone.

Alex

Katie is losing it. Who ever thought I'd want my mother to whip out her shrink index cards again?

I call her today, and she's a mess. She rambles about Julie and that Marissa bitch.

"Baby," I say. I keep my voice low and steady, like they do on TV when talking to hysterical people. "Baby, just ignore it. You didn't do anything."

She's crying. "I did," she says. "I did. I told you—"

I tune her out. I remember what she told me, and I don't want to hear about her and some other guy again. What she did or didn't do. I pound my fist on my night table. Cheap piece of shit cracks. I take a deep breath. "It's not the end of the world, okay? It's just words. Call her a whore back. I'm sure you wouldn't be the first."

I think I hear a snort come through the cries, like she laughed or something. But then she starts with the crying again. Fuck. Guys wouldn't be bawling now. They'd go punch someone. I pound the night table again, and it breaks in two.

"Hang in there, baby. I'll see you soon. I'll drive up at the end of the week."

She sniffles. "That would be good."

I keep her on the phone and talk quietly, telling her it will be okay. Her breathing slows down, and I think she's asleep.

"I'll see you soon," I say.

"Alex?" she says, voice sleepy.

"Yeah?"

"Whatever happens, remember I'm really sorry. And I never cared about anyone like I do about you."

"Just get some sleep. Nothing's going to happen," I say, and hang up.

Julie

School is out for the day, and I'm halfway home before I realize I left my study sheet in Mr. Stevens's homeroom. I run back, cursing myself for being stupid. The halls are silent, and it doesn't feel as safe without Chloe. His door is open, but only a crack. I hear arguing and look inside. I see cheerleader shoes, and I just know they're Marissa's, but I peek anyway to make sure. It *is* her. The voices get louder and I press myself against the lockers. Is this her secret? She failing science or something?

But that's not what they're arguing about. "Sleeping with her again!" I hear her say. "You told me it was over." He tells her to keep her voice down. I can't be hearing this right. I get closer to the door. "It doesn't mean anything, I swear," he says, like from a clichéd movie. Marissa cries, and I don't feel bad. "I'm sorry, baby," says Mr. Stevens. Then there's silence. I get closer, my heart pounding. They're kissing. His hand goes up her leg, and I don't stay to see more.

On the way home, I'm bursting to tell Chloe. I don't think about Mr. Stevens. Only him and Marissa. Marissa and her red marker. Marissa smearing the stalls with Katie's name. Marissa looking so smug. Marissa looking at Katie like *she's* the whore. God, who's the whore now, bitch?

I start to text Chloe as soon as I get home, but my thoughts are running faster than my fingers. I call her and she can't believe it. I tell her in detail what I saw. She wants me to tell it again and we dissect the whole thing. Over and over and over.

"Guess they're going to have to change all the names in the stall to Marissa now," says Chloe.

We're silent, and we get the idea at the same time. We text everyone we know.

Katie

Julie runs into my room. She tells me what she saw. She tells me what she did.

"Tell me you didn't!" I feel the floor shake. I don't know why Julie is not shaking with it.

"You should be thanking me, not yelling at me. She won't call you names anymore."

"You don't know what you started."

"What?" she screams. "What did I start?"

But I can't tell her because the sound from the earth cracking is too loud.

Julie

The next day, it's all over the school. Marissa gets called down to the office. Katie should be doing cartwheels, but she goes home sick.

No one can talk about anything except the "rumors," but Chloe and I know they're not rumors. In History we talk about being innocent until proven guilty. Our teacher throws up her hands. "Forget this. Who thinks he did it?"

We look at each other and raise our hands. She does too.

Katie

I hear Marissa's name on the intercom, and my stomach churns.

Ethan bloodies his hand on a row of lockers.

I run to the bathroom to throw up. The trees I drew before look bolder and brighter but new words are creeping through the leaves every second.

I go to the school nurse and tell her I'm sick. She calls my mother, who says I'm allowed to walk home. I gather my things quickly and sprint to the doors. Marissa is there, like she knew I'd be making an escape.

"I warned you," she hisses.

"It wasn't me."

Her eyes are glassy. "I don't care how they know, but they know. And he confirmed it. Just like that." She snaps her fingers. "What the hell was all the secrecy for if he was going to break so easily?"

I'm desperate. "So, see? He admitted it. It's over."

"You're so stupid. What do you think everyone is going to be saying about me now? What about Ethan?"

Her mom drives up. "You take care, Katie," Marissa says, getting in the car.

They begin to drive away when the car stops. Marissa opens her window. "Be sure to check your messages. I'll be sending you something special."

Kyle

You sit in the kitchen and stare at the television. A school right over the border, East High, in Cherry Hill. Julie and Katie's school. Teacher-student affair.

You don't hear Alex come up behind you until he says, "Crazy shit, right?"

You have a bad feeling about this. Your mouth is dry. He doesn't notice.

"You know what the fucked-up thing about all this is?" He heats up a slice of leftover pizza. You shake your head no when he offers to heat a slice up for you too. "The fucked-up thing is, the girl is probably some slut. She probably wanted it as much as he did, but she's a minor." He puts air quotes around the word minor. The microwave beeps and he takes out his slice. "Now, I bet the dude's career is done. All because of some ho." He takes a bite. "You'll see I'm right, because what do I always tell you?"

He looks at you like he wants an answer. You find your voice. "Stay away from hos."

He slaps you on the back. "Fuck yeah. Stay away from dirty hos."

Katie

Marissa is absent all week, Mr. Strum is too, but we know he's not coming back. I check my messages like an addict, but nothing comes up. Marissa's name rivals mine in the stalls.

By the end of the week, I can almost breathe again. Julie bounces through the halls like she's prom queen. Leah says she always knew Marissa would have made an awful Pyramid Girl. Ethan stops coming to our lunch table. He looks like he hasn't slept in days. Friday after school, he walks past me in the hall, and I speed up to get further away from him.

"Wait! Please," he calls.

I stop.

"Why did she do it?" he asks when I get closer. "Why?" He doesn't wait for me to answer. "And you know what else? I lost my fucking cell. All in one damn week."

He looks through me and walks away, still mumbling about his lost cell and how the world has it in for him. And why does he always get the cheaters?

When I walk home, the earth doesn't rumble. The voices

are barely a whisper. By the time I get in the door, I am almost calm. I check my messages again, and for the first time this week I'm sure nothing will come up. I smile and text Alex I'm turning in early.

Love you, babe, he texts back, and I fall asleep.

Julie

The text comes from Chloe. She sends me to a link on a private server. I want to throw up. I go on Facebook. Link after link after link with my name: *See @Julie Taylor's sister HERE* posted on my friends' pages.

Marissa's page is public, and she doesn't stop at the link. She embeds the video. There's one line: *WHO'S THE WHORE NOW?*

Kyle

You get bombarded with texts and emails and Facebook messages.

You're watching the video like it's a pileup. Alex isn't home yet, but there's no way he doesn't know. And if he doesn't, it's only a matter of time.

"Did you see?" Julie asks when you pick up your phone.

"I'm watching it now."

Silence. Then, "Can you *stop* watching it?"

You do.

"How could she do *that*?" asks Julie.

"She doesn't look like she likes it." Maybe Julie can't tell, but you can. The way her body is rigid, the leer on the guys' faces, her blank eyes.

Julie snorts. "Did you see the whole thing? She's smiling. The. Whole. Time. She even says it feels good."

You know it didn't. "Maybe they made her."

"I thought—" Julie's voice catches and she takes a deep breath. "I thought, when I called, you'd be there for *me*. I thought you'd find a way to make me feel better."

Downstairs the door slams. You close and lock the door to your room. In the room next door, you hear banging and cursing. Something breaks. He heard.

"I have to go," you say, voice shaking.

"That's it? That's all you have?"

He pounds on your door. You put your dresser against it.

"Kyle?" Julie says, her voice shrill. "KYLE!"

"Maybe it wasn't her fault," you say, and hang up.

Julie

I hang up the phone. Is Katie still sleeping? I knock on her door, but she doesn't answer.

I knock harder and harder and harder. "Just go away," she finally says.

I want to scream at her and ask her why she did it. Then I want to scream and ask her why she didn't tell me. If she had just told me what she was afraid of—if she had just told me *this* might be out there—I would have run out of that school and kept on running. I would have told no one about Marissa.

This is out because of me. And I hate that. And it's out because she was too scared to tell me. To own up that she wasn't so perfect.

For that, I hate her more.

Katie

The weekend passes, and the video is still there. Not the video I erased. That's gone. This one is worse. This is of that afternoon. The afternoon I thought I was ending it all. The afternoon I did everything they wanted while smiling like I loved it. I'm everywhere now. Not on Facebook anymore because the higher-ups removed it, but copies exist. On people's phones, in their hard drives, on that private Internet site. Lots of people comment. I don't read what they say, just check if more come in.

The principal, Mr. Jenkins, paid us a house call minutes ago, saying he personally is taking measures to make sure the video doesn't circulate further. They're working on taking it off the Internet, but these things take time. He tells my parents he's certain, since we're all minors, that appropriate authorities will be involved. I can tell he doesn't really know what the charges will be. "Of course," he says, "the boys will be punished." Until they undergo psychological counseling, "to begin immediately," he says, Chris and

Ethan are suspended from the remaining baseball games, summer football practice, and football season.

I laugh. My mother's head snaps in my direction. "I hardly think this is a laughing matter, young lady."

"But it is. They'll be done with counseling by the time football starts. And baseball has, what, four games left?"

Mr. Jenkins shifts uncomfortably. "If more counseling is required, they will receive it. They will learn their lesson."

My father's face is red. "And of course those summer practices are so necessary. Wouldn't want the 'boys' to miss them." His voice oozes sarcasm and I laugh again. And again. And again.

"Control yourself," my mother hisses.

My father grasps my hand. He squeezes hard until I calm down, until my laughter is replaced by sobbing. Sobbing not loud enough to drown out the voices around me.

"What if we want to press charges?" he says.

My mother gasps in horror. "We will not be pressing charges."

"What if we want to press charges?" my father asks, louder.

My mother smiles so wide, she looks like the Joker. "Jerry," she says in her placating voice.

My father begins again, in a voice so booming I jump. "What—"

"The police can talk to you about those options," says Mr. Jenkins. "But I do advise you to think long and hard about that. The boys feel terrible. It's their senior year next year. There are scouts already eyeing them. Do we really want to ruin their futures for one mistake?"

"No," says my mother. "We do not. There will be no charges."

"Anna!"

I watch them argue back and forth, watch Mr. Jenkins shift this way and that, a cross between boredom and impatience. I forget who they are talking about. I forget that I'm involved in this at all. Who are these awful boys? Who is this girl my mother is calling "not such a victim," this girl who "didn't even say no," "didn't fight back," who "said she liked it, for heaven's sake." Mr. Jenkins tells my parents that at least "the boys are cooperating." That at least they're talking. Katie is not talking. She refuses to answer questions. "From the video ... " Mr. Jenkins clears his throat, turns red, clears his throat again. "From the video, it appears she was a willing participant."

My phone vibrates. A text from Alex. The first since this happened. I block out their voices and check the text.

FUCKING LYING WHORE.

It's all I need to see.

"There will be no charges," I whisper, and leave the room.

Julie

Chloe gets permission to ditch her classes and go to mine instead. Same teachers, different periods, so not that hard. She stays close to me, arm around my shoulder, just daring anyone to say something. They do, of course. But it's easier with her there.

What's not easy is seeing Katie walk like a zombie through the halls. Guys push her against lockers. Someone snaps at the waistband of her pants, and she keeps walking. No fight at all, like she doesn't give a crap.

Someone spray-painted *WHORE* on her locker. The janitors have given up trying to scrub it off. I told her to spray-paint over it. To ask for a locker change. To do *something*. She looked at me, then at her locker like the words were new to her. She ran her finger over them. Then walked away.

When someone asks me if I think she knew she was being taped, I don't have an answer. When someone asks why she did it, I don't know either. She didn't fight back then, she's not fighting back now. She could have wanted it. Maybe that's why she's keeping the locker as is. It's payback.

"Ignore them," Chloe says. "Just think of Kyle."

Yep, I've *been* thinking of him. Of his newest text: Hang in there. Talk about warm and fuzzy. I don't tell Chloe that; I just let her gush about how awesome he is and how super-duper lucky I am to have him.

"Ignore him, too," says Chloe in my ear, pointing at Derek and his posse of asses. I would not have even noticed him if she hadn't pointed him out.

They're laughing and high-fiving him and they're all making disgusting gestures with their hands and mouth. I don't have to hear them to know they're talking about Katie. And then Derek points at me and he whispers something to his buddies and they all crack up again.

Then he calls out to me. He hasn't spoken to me since he called it quits, and he's yelling for me now. Motioning for me to come over. I stick my middle finger up at him.

"Oooh, tough girl. You trying to say you miss me?"

"Just keep walking," Chloe says. She knows if I stop, it won't end well. She knows how I can get.

"Yeah, you walk away," yells Derek. "But when you're ready to have a little more of this"—he grabs his crotch—"you know where to find me."

His group of idiots laughs. My face is red. He made me care about him, screwed me over, and now has the balls to say *that*. No.

"Walk, Julie, walk."

But I don't. I open my mouth to say something bad. Something hurtful. But the words come too quickly. "No, asshole. I think you're confusing me with my sister."

Katie

The school counselor
gives me:
pamphlets
a pep talk
her number
other extracurriculars to explore now that I'm not
       Pyramid Girl
"I'm here if you need me. You need someone."
Maybe I don't

Julie
has stopped:
asking me to fight back
coming into my room
wanting to hear my side
"People are thinking you wanted this.
       ARE like this."
Maybe I am

Alex
calls:
me words that have lost all meaning
to cry
to say he doesn't know why I lied to him
to tell me he could have done it rough
"Is that what you wanted?"
Maybe I did

Mama
tells me:
she warned me
who's going to want me now
I can forget about being prom queen
Heck, I can forget about going to prom at all
"I don't understand you. I thought you wanted
     all that.
Those princess dresses.
A fine princess you'll be now! We'll fix it."
Maybe I don't want her to fix it

Daddy
says:
This changes nothing
I'm beautiful
Men are pigs
"Don't cry, baby. Don't cry."

Kyle
texts:
your eyes looked empty
are U OK?

They all say:
"Say something, Katie."
"Goddamnit, Katie."
"Fucking say something!"
"Are you there?"
"Are you there?"
"Are you there?"
No.
Maybe I never was.

Julie

Three weeks left of school, and Mama tells me Katie is starting her summer early. "Don't be angry, Julie. I know it's not fair, but you'll be at the lake house soon enough."

Angry? No way. It's like I've been granted my wish. She's been slowly disappearing anyway. Not speaking, clothes using her body as merely a hanger. It's like she's been a ghost, but not quite. A walking dead girl. A constant reminder that gets the rumors and taunts going. A constant source of arguing for my parents. Like a tornado that wreaks havoc but keeps going, oblivious to the damage it left behind.

People get bored quickly in my school, especially if there's no one to hear them. I hug my mother out of relief, and she stumbles back, surprised. Then, "I don't think I tell you enough what a good girl you are."

Enough? Try at all.

"How's Kyle doing?" Her tone actually sounds interested.

"Great," I say, which is a lie, but this conversation is going well.

Truth is, things are tense with Kyle. I can't even say Katie's name without getting bombarded by a verbal diarrhea of concern. For *her*. When I tell him the things people say to me, I know, even when he doesn't say it, that he's thinking poor Katie has it worse, poor Katie has to experience all of this. All of what? Do we even know if she's upset because it happened, or just because the footage got out? Nope. She hasn't talked. And, if she just lay there and let shit happen to her without fighting back, without trying to clear her own name, why should the rest of us waste our energy feeling sorry for her and defending her?

"You know what we should do? Go to the mall and get you some new summer clothes to wow him. Whatever you want. How's that sound? Show that boy just how lucky he really is."

I pinch myself, and it hurts. This is real. If Mama and I can work, surely Kyle and I can, too.

| Summer |

Kyle

~ The Lake House ~

If it weren't for your grandparents wanting to see you and Alex, you'd have skipped the lake house this year. Too much has happened. It's not a break anymore. Not relaxing. Not fun. You can't go back to playing Spit with Julie, not like before. When she spits on the ground now, you'll be too focused on watching her mouth, remembering where it's been, what it's said.

She's trying, you'll give her that. Maybe spending time with her Ice Queen mother has changed her, but she told you she gets it now. Gets that Katie must be in pain. Gets that people saying things to *her* was a way to get back at Katie. And you gave in, too. You told her that no one should have said anything to her. That she doesn't deserve that. That you understand the last two months haven't been easy for her, either. That last sentence makes her giddy, silly, so happy. Like last summer's Julie, like a Julie who cares about other people and not just herself. But there's something between the two of you that's changed and can't be fixed. All you did was give Katie a break, and it's as if you committed a sin.

Then there's Alex. Who couldn't wait to get on the road. Who's jumping out of his skin to get to the lake house. Who never brought a parade of girls home, even after the video. He broke things. He cursed. He screamed. He probably got some somewhere. But he left you alone.

Right after *it* hit the Internet, you kept your door locked. You avoided Alex's room, didn't even join him in the kitchen. But there wasn't a need. Soon, you accepted the comforting silence. Now he's humming to the radio, tapping to the beat on the steering wheel, enjoying the feel of the open windows.

You're almost at the Catskills when he says, "We're cool now, Katie and I. So, if you were staying away from Julie for my sake, you don't have to."

"You're cool? I thought she was a ho."

"Yeah, well, so is every other girl. I think I can get past it. We'll see what happens." He smiles too big. You feel him glance in your direction. You don't check to be sure. That feeling you used to get in the pit of your stomach is back. You turn the radio up loud to block out his humming.

Soon, you're pulling onto the gravel path. Your grandparents are waiting by the cottage, huge grins, squeezing each other's hands. So happy to see you. Alex parks the car and sprints to them, giving them a big hug. His smile doesn't waver. The skip in his step seems real. You plaster a smile on your face and let your grandmother pinch your cheeks. You look at the girls' cottage. Just darkness. Julie is not coming until tomorrow. You wonder how Katie is.

Grandma leads both of you in, talking nonstop about the pies she baked, the spread that's waiting on the table. Alex kisses her cheek. "Thank God. I'm starving."

"What about you?" she asks, looking past your smile like she always can. Like your dad always could. "Something?"

You nod and pick at a baked apple, normally a favorite. Alex wasn't kidding about his need to eat. He inhales sandwiches, fruit, bread, soup. Your grandparents laugh, so pleased. But you know better. It's only a matter of time until you find out. The apple sits in your stomach, and you can feel its skin, seeds, all of it, shaping itself whole again.

Katie

I've spent three weeks just lying in bed with the shades drawn. When Babushka brings me food, she sits beside me while I eat but doesn't ask any questions. After the first week, I ask her why she doesn't. Doesn't she want to know what really happened? She strokes my hair and tells me she knows. Knows me inside and out, I don't have to tell her anything. So I save my voice for Alex, because I know he'll want to know everything I can explain and can't.

Week two, Babushka and I play cards, and I help her cook. In the evenings, I go down to the creek myself and throw stones. Week three, Dedushka says I still spend too much alone time. It's isn't good for me. So every morning, I wake before sunrise, put on sweatpants and flannels, and go berry-picking with him. We watch the sun rise together, pick more berries, and bring them home for Babushka. Dedushka tells me to listen to the animals while we pick, to listen to the creek, to the sun leaving the clouds. Dedushka tells me he hasn't seen me swing, and the two of us walk to the swings and swing high. He tells me to listen to the swings—

the higher I swing, the louder the swings will cheer. *Listen*, he keeps repeating. The way he says it, it's like he knows there are other voices trying to break through. I do what he says. I spend my last week of solitude listening. And soon the voices are barely a whisper.

Julie

··The Chickens·

Only two days here, and already it's chicken time! I feel my adrenaline pumping. The squawking gets louder as the pickup speeds over the gravel, sending bits of rock flying toward the cottages. I feel one scrape my cheek and wince. Dust gets in my eyes. I rub them and when I move my hands, Alex is by my side.

"Shit, what's that?" He grabs hold of my chin and turns my face towards him. I try to pull away and he holds tighter. "That's a nasty cut. You got peroxide?"

I'm shocked by his concern. "Uh, in the bathroom." He follows me inside, and I hand him the bottle and cotton.

He soaks the cotton in peroxide and rubs it across my cheek. It stings and I jump. "Hold still," he says, then rummages in the medicine cabinet for a Band-Aid. He puts it on my cheek, surprisingly gentle. "God," he says, "what's with the doe eyes? The gash was making me yak."

I turn red. Not like I like him. Just nice of him, that's all.

And, yeah, he's hot, but Kyle—even with the recent weird-ness—is more my speed. Even if he wasn't, Alex is Katie's. Kyle tells me he thinks they're going to work things out. So I guess, tainted or not, she's still better than me.

"No one is making eyes at you," I snap. "I just never saw this side of you before. Uh, what would you call it? Oh yeah. Human."

"Whatever." He's already heading toward the lake house door. "We're missing the chickens."

I run after him, and we get out in time to see the knife cut through a feathered neck. My cheek throbs. This chicken doesn't fly. It just flops straight to the ground. Alex shakes his head, disappointed.

"Right?" I say. "Like, where's the show?"

I hear the faint sound of swings in the distance and know Katie and Kyle are on them. I hate that they're together. I hate that they're both so … so weak. No, just Katie. Not Kyle. I push the thought out of my head, but Alex grabs it.

"I guess we're the ones with the balls."

I try to sound tough. "If you don't have balls, they walk all over you."

"True dat." He nods appreciatively and gives me a fist bump. We stare at each other a beat too long.

Screaming. People move back. Flailing legs knock over benches.

The squeak of swings stops.

"What the fuck?" shouts Alex, and I see that our clothes are splattered with blood.

The butcher is embarrassed. He apologizes to everyone.

I notice it's not Wilbur. His name tag reads *Brett*. Poor Brett. But he had to know "Bretts" are not made to kill chickens. To model shirts with a chicken logo, maybe, but not to kill them while wearing old, stinky overalls. Brett tells everyone they can get a chicken for half price and if they buy two, they'll get a third free. Everyone still has blood on them, but the discount calms the masses.

"Shit. Way to ruin a good time."

"Yeah, but I feel a little bad for him, you know? What are the odds he'll be back again?"

Alex snorts. "Not my problem. Guy should know how to do his job."

In the distance, the swings start up again. They seem to be louder and faster this time, working double to block out the noise from seconds ago.

The butcher picks up another chicken. This one's brown with a little red dome. It flaps its wings while the man holds its legs. I look at Alex. He's leaning forward, almost salivating. The chicken flaps harder and I feel sick. I want to be brave. Because Katie isn't. Mama said the other day that I was strong. I had those kinds of eyes. She said she never had strong eyes. She said she never noticed it before, but Katie's eyes are shaped like my father's. I wondered whose eyes I have, then. It didn't matter, though, because I have something Mama wanted.

Squeak, squeak, squeak. I picture the swing really high in the air. I wonder if I'd have the guts to jump off.

The knife slices clean. The wings stop flapping, and the chicken drops to the ground, not even a twitch.

"Bullshit," mumbles Alex.

"Totally," I say, but my heart is beating quickly and the sound of the swings is hurting my eardrums.

"What's the matter with you? I think you've been spending too much time with Kyle."

The ground spins. "Shut up."

Alex laughs. He squeezes my knee. "Chicks. You're all the same."

But I'm not. I block out the noise of the swings. The squawks of the chickens. The clucking of the grandparents. Just focus my eyes on the knife as it slices through one throat after another. Chicken after chicken falls on the ground. I hate them all for not fighting back.

Katie

Alex has been here three days and still no word. But I think we will talk tonight. I think he's psyching himself up. And the chickens were here yesterday. He's always in a better mood after the chickens.

I try to psyche myself up, too, to rehearse what I'll say, but it's hard to think. Especially with Julie's blood-stained shirt lying at the foot of my bed. I don't think it was an accident. It's still here because I refuse to touch it. Last night I dreamt I slept in a grave of bloody carcasses. I couldn't catch my breath, woke up sweating. The only comforting part of the dream was that the pit was warm.

It's dark outside now, and I can feel him coming. Then I hear him. His familiar knock of "Shave and a Haircut" on the screen door. I whip open the door and run into his arms without thinking. It's been so long. He doesn't pull away. Not immediately. But then he's rigid, like he just remembered this was a different girl than the one from summers past.

"We should talk," he says, and takes my hand.

I nod too eagerly, so happy he's still willing to hold my hand.

We walk to the creek in silence, and when we get there, he walks to the rocks and starts skimming them on the water. I don't feel like joining in and prolonging the inevitable. "Talk," I call over to him. My voice startles him and his rock falls into the water, creating a big splash. "Sorry," I mumble. But not for him to hear, just for me to try out the word in my mouth again, to see if it means anything anymore, if it sounds any different from overuse.

He sits beside me on the grass and taps my toe with his. "Where do we go from here?"

I raise my chin to look at him, and there's something different about his face that I can't pinpoint. He looks exactly the same, but there's a lip twitch that wasn't there before, a darkening of the eyes . . . not necessarily sinister, more like a shadow, a blackness that covers what his eyes used to be, a curtain hiding the real Alex.

"I think that's up to you, isn't it?" I say.

He rips chunks of grass and throws them in the direction of the lake. "Why just me? There's nothing you want to say?"

I feel heat in my toes. My fists clench. When I lay in the dark of the cottage, I thought of a million different ways I would apologize to him again. New ways to explain, but he didn't want to hear any of it before.

"I'll listen," he says, as if reading my mind.

I take a deep breath and tell him everything. What Pyramid Girl Katie's life was, the party, the alcohol, the bed, Ethan then Chris, how I thought I said no, the pain, the flashes.

He puts his hand up as a stop sign. Gets up, grabs a big rock, and throws it far into the creek. He punches a tree. He screams. "Fuck! You were drunk. They shouldn't have done that when you were drunk. Fuck!" He mumbles to himself, like he's struggling with the images. I get that. I still do. Then he stops, looks at me. "But I saw the video. You weren't drunk in the video."

I bite my lip, shake my head no. His eyes flash Jasmine hate. He turns away from me but doesn't leave. Finally, he says, "Say everything you want to say." But he still doesn't turn around.

I tell him about how Chris wouldn't leave me alone, what he kept doing, how I slept with him again to keep him away.

He puts his face in his hands. "You let me think ... I thought ... I waited ... fucking A." He paces. Throws another rock. His knuckles are bleeding, and I walk toward him. He's not looking at me, but he hears me. "Don't touch me right now," he says. "Please."

I sit back down and wait for him to tell me he's ready to hear more.

"Go on."

I say that the summer *after* saved me, *he* saved me, our first time was *real*, *he*—no one else—was the best I ever had. I hear his breath come our jagged. Is he crying? I can't get up and look. I can't see his eyes. I want to. I don't.

"Go on."

I tell him about that afternoon at my locker, how they showed me a video of that night, how they said they'd make it go away. How I followed them and did what they wanted and how they hurt me. How I did everything for us (or was it me?), how I had no idea they'd recorded everything again. How I didn't, I didn't, I *didn't* like it.

There's silence. He turns around. "The *first* time"— he counts off on his fingers—"you were out of your mind drunk. You slept with two of them. You probably said no, or tried to."

He gets it. I'm relieved. "I did."

"Just be quiet. The *second* time"—he raises two fingers— "you weren't drunk, but you wanted one of them to go away, so you fucked him."

I flinch. He looks at me like he wants confirmation. I nod slowly.

"And you don't tell me about any of it. But you know what? I can almost get that. I fucked my share before that summer."

He's scaring me. This is not my summer boy. This isn't the Alex/Sasha I think I know.

He walks closer to me, stops himself, and goes back to the tree again. "What I don't get is that after you and I did it— after I do everything for you, things I never did for anyone else—after I give up all the bitches back home, you fuck the both of them *again*. You say you did that for *us*? Where was *I*? I don't remember getting shit out of this."

The tears are flowing down my cheeks and I gulp back more. I can't see his eyes through my tears. "You hate me," I whisper, and get up to leave. I hate me too.

"No." He comes to me and pulls me toward him and kisses me deep, like he's trying to get out anything I may not have told him, expose more than I let on. But there's nothing else. He pulls away like he's disgusted, with himself and me both. "I've tried but I can't. What the hell does that say about me?"

"That means we have a chance. I can still fix it."

His eyes are black. "It's worth a shot."

"Anything," I say.

"I know the perfect spot," he says, walking up the hill, toward the dumpsters. I shiver but I follow.

He pushes me down on the grass, and I pull him to me. He pulls at my hair. His hands grip my arms too tightly, and it hurts. I bite my lip to stop from screaming, and he pulls at my pants.

He rips my shirt and squeezes my breasts too tight. I know he knows he's hurting me, but I say nothing and he doesn't stop. The smell of rotted chicken carcasses seeps through the dumpsters and fills my nose, and I keep my mouth shut tight to stop myself from throwing up.

He pushes inside me, pounding, pushing my head against the cold dumpster. I try not to think about the pieces of chicken flesh coating it and bite my lip harder. When he's done, he pulls up his pants and walks away.

We're even now.

Kyle

You didn't avoid her last week. Not really. You said hello, gave her a hug, played a game of Spit. Then Brett came and you watched her and Alex salivating over those chickens. You saw him sit too close. You saw him touch her knee. She never flinched. She used to flinch. Whenever he'd go near her, she'd scare. Repel. Not anymore. You're not thinking she's into him, not like *that*, but it's something. And there was that moment, before the screams and the blood, where it seemed like the two of them fused together.

You wanted to ask Katie if she'd seen it, but she wasn't looking at them. Just mouthing something with her lips. You think it may have been "listen."

But you can't keep (not) avoiding her, so you go where you know Julie will be, where she's been every morning waiting for you but pretending she wasn't. Sitting on the bench in front of her cottage, cards in hand, playing Solitaire. You see her glance up from her cards and see you and then look back down pretending she didn't, trying not to smile. You don't want to be that guy, that guy she has to play games with, the guy she has to retreat from.

"Hey," you say, sitting down across from her. You reach for the cards, and she hands them to you.

"Hey."

You shuffle. "Spit?"

Her mouth moves like she's going to spit on the ground like she used to. Your mouth moves too. Neither of you do it. "Sure."

"How've you been?"

Her eyes flash, hopeful, when you lead with this. "I've been. How about you?"

You shrug. "I've been better."

"Yeah." She takes the deck you hand her and places four cards on the bench. "Spit."

Then you both look only at the cards. Hands flick one on top of another, faster and faster. Fingers grasp the cards from the palm and throw them on the bench and the center piles. She finishes first and grabs the smaller pile like this is the only mission she has. "In your face, yo!"

You laugh, but she says it too vehemently, like she would mash the cards into your skin if she could. Maybe your face shows this because she says softly, "Sorry."

You put your hand on hers. She doesn't move it away, but you swear she flinches.

"Why have you been avoiding me?" she asks.

You want to say you haven't, but you're not lying to her. "I was figuring things out."

"And have you?"

"I think so." You squeeze her hand.

"Good." She tucks her hair behind her ear. "Can I tell you something without you getting mad?"

You nod, even though you know this will lead nowhere good.

She shuffles the cards and separates them into two piles. "I was scared about coming here."

"Why?" You choose a pile.

"It was easier, without Katie at home and at school. Like nothing had happened." She's leaning forward like she's telling you this huge secret, like she's sharing this piece of herself, except—this isn't really about her. But as you've noticed these last few months, everything is somehow about Julie.

You don't want to hear this. "And how is it now?"

She shrugs. "I haven't really talked to her. What's there to say?"

"Your turn," you say, motioning to the piles of cards.

She cocks her head like she's expecting a bigger reaction from you. "You're never really going to see it from my side, are you?" Her face contorts, her lip curls back. She looks nothing like the Julie you once knew. She looks mean, like her bite could kill.

"Why does there have to be a 'side'? It's not enough that I get you're upset?"

She shuffles her pile of cards. "What do you and Katie talk about on the swings?"

You blink in surprise. She's jealous. How did you not see this before? "You, of course."

Her face goes back to normal. She smiles. "It would be cool if you could watch with me sometime."

You pale. "The butchering? No thanks."

She snorts. "I guess Alex and I have more balls than either of you."

You put the cards back on the bench. She's even talking like him. "I'll see you later."

She jumps up. "What the hell? Can't you take a joke?"

You keep walking.

"Why do you have to be such a baby?" Her voice goes up an octave.

You hear her running behind you. Then she's in front of you, making you look at her.

"I'm sorry," she says. You can almost see the Julie that helped you breathe. "I don't know why I said that. Please come back. Please?"

Her eyes tear, and they look like they used to—but not quite. "Please?" she says again.

You sigh and let her lead you back.

Alex

How can I believe that she didn't like giving that guy head? That she didn't like one of them fucking her? How can I believe that, when she didn't even struggle? When she just lay there? When her head bobbed up and down and her hand moved just so, just like she does it with me? And how, even after I bang her up a little, she keeps coming back, wanting to be with me? Wouldn't that mean she liked it with them too?

Julie

I hear the swings stop and know she'll be in our room within minutes. I get into bed and turn out the light. The darkness makes me anxious, but at least I won't have to see her when she comes in.

She turns on the light as soon as she enters, making that impossible. "Hi."

I fake grogginess. "No, you didn't wake me. Thanks for asking."

She stares at me like she's preparing a speech—I can't tell if it's one of prosecution or defense—then slightly shakes her head and sighs. "I'm sorry."

Her voice is tired, like those words drained the little energy she had left. I feel bad. "Forget it."

She turns away from me and stares at the mirror, nudging her face against the glass and pulling at the skin under her eyes. Even in the dim lighting I can see a darkening there. My curiosity gets the best of me. "When was the last time you slept?"

"I sleep."

Not much. I prop myself on an elbow. "It happened. It's over. We should all move on." I overheard Daddy saying this to Mama a few weeks ago when she was in her Katie-bashing mood. It sounds mature. I like feeling like the sensible adult.

Katie finally turns around to face me. "Really?" Her voice is full of fake cheer. "Is that how everyone feels? Well, by all means, let's move on, Jules."

She plops herself on my bed and pats me on my blanket-covered legs. "Let's catch up, sweet sister of mine!" Her voice is octaves higher than normal. "What would you like to share with me? Hmm?"

"There's nothing to share," I mumble.

"No? How's Kyle? Oh, that's right. We can't talk about him. He's awful because he was willing to be my friend."

His name from her mouth gives me hives. How do I explain that? It's just another betrayal. Another boy choosing her over me.

"He likes you." She stands up. "You can't blame me for whatever is going on with you two."

I turn away from her, and she turns off the lights and heads back outside, slamming the door behind her.

I want to follow her. I don't want to follow her. What would I say? It was my fault the tape came out? I'm sorry, but hating you has become so easy that stopping would leave me empty?

Kyle

You pull the swing back, back, back, but no matter how far you go, you can't block out the bloodbath by the lake houses.

"I'm done," Katie says. "Where can we go to escape?"

If you had more balls, you'd take Alex's car and go for a drive, but knight-on-a-horse has never been you. "I know just the place," you say. You walk with her to the end of the lake house properties. You like to go there alone, far from the cottages, and hide out in a cloak of trees.

"And the irony," you hear Katie saying, "is that they're all males."

"What? Who?"

"The chickens. I always thought they were girls, but no. I bet Alex doesn't know."

"There's no way he'd watch if he did."

"They castrate them before they're killed, too. Or else a rush of testosterone fills their muscles when they're slaughtered and the taste is changed." She looks sick and fascinated at the same time.

"How do you know all this?" You're almost by the trees.

"My old bio teacher, the one from the news? He was totally obsessed with poultry. Did his PhD in the field. The class was right after lunch. Lost a lot of weight that year." She laughs.

"We're here," you say when you get to the clearing. You watch her face to see the reaction. It opens, all greenness gone.

"Wow, it's better than the creek."

This makes you proud and warm. Then she says, "Has Julie seen it?"

She hasn't. Why have you never brought her here? "Not yet."

"I won't tell her I've been here, then."

You stare at her. "She'd care?" But even as the words leave your mouth, you know the answer. Of course she would. So, again, why haven't you asked her first? Was it just the timing? And now it's too late?

"A lot," says Katie. You can tell she's thinking. Her fingers lace into each other, and then she sighs. "I can't be here with you."

She begins walking back, and you follow. You don't talk as you head for the swings. The squawking is still going when you get closer to the cottages.

"I can't take this," she says.

You get one more idea. "Follow me." You lead her to the road outside. Cars swoosh by quickly, and you crowd the small strip of pavement too close to the road. But here, you can't hear anything but the cars. Drivers stick up their middle fingers and honk, but it's heaven.

Katie smiles and closes her eyes.

Katie

The passing cars remind me of South Street. I stand here at night because it's loudest. Sometimes Kyle is with me. I watched his face once, and he looked blank, but not in a bad way. Like the sounds erased everything in his head, and his body was just a placeholder for the real person inside. He saw me watching and turned his back to me. I didn't look at him after that, but I liked that I saw that about him. It made me feel sad for him, but also less alone.

I'm staring at the lights as they whizz by. The energy fills the road and reaches my toes. SWOOSH, SWOOSH, SWOOSH. One car after another. I close my eyes and wonder what it would feel like to step in front of them. Would the energy surge through me and make me invincible again? Would it make the voices shouting *Whore, Bitch, Skank, Slut* disappear? Would Ethan and Chris stop haunting me forever, appearing everywhere I go?

The voices. The faces. They're no longer a whisper. They're full-on three dimensional. They're loud and brazen. The first time they screamed was after Alex and I "made up."

Each day, they gain power. I listen to the sun, to the animals, to the moon, to the swings. I listen really hard, like Dedushka told me, but it's not helping. Probably because I keep going back to Alex. They're loudest with him.

But I need to keep going back, for the glimpses. Those glimpses of love I catch in his eyes. They might be there for only a split second, but they're there. And I keep thinking, if I just stay with him longer, that love will grow to what it was. All I have to do is get it to the surface.

Until then, I keep returning to the cars. I think the lights and sounds make me stronger. Even if they don't, they're loud enough to keep the voices low.

Kyle

You listen for the screech of the swings. That's how you know Alex is done with her and she's there. Sometimes you find her by the cars, but she's been saying they haven't been enough anymore. She needs the swings, too. The worst nights are when the screeching goes on for hours, and you wonder what she's thinking. Does she want him to come out and join her? He never does. Sometimes he's in your room watching TV. Other times his car is gone and you can only assume he's out finding new girls to fill the noise in his head left over from the screeching. Or is he over her already? The video proved his point, and he's moved on? Even Alex is not like that. He wishes he could move on, but you think Katie has invaded his brain.

Tonight the swings cry louder than usual, later than usual. It's cold outside, and you grab a sweatshirt for her because you're sure she doesn't have one with her. Julie nags your thoughts, but this isn't betrayal. You're just saving the weak. Julie doesn't need saving.

You walk through the grass. It's cold and wet and overdue

for a mow. You watch her as you walk closer. Her legs push hard and fierce, and you can't see her expression, but you can only assume it's the same. When you're almost beside her, she notices you and slows down. Her shoulders slump and there's no fierceness at all. You sit beside her and absently move the sweatshirt between your fingers. It doesn't seem that cold anymore.

She shivers. "Are you going to wear that?" She nods at the sweatshirt.

You shake your head no. "Good," she says. "I'm freezing." She takes the sweatshirt from your hands and pulls it over her head, her long-sleeved tee rising over her belly, revealing too-thin curves and fresh, blue bruises. As if remembering, she pulls the sweatshirt down quickly.

"It's not polite to stare," she says. She's a different Katie than she was before the tape. Emptier. Or pretending to be.

She's wearing capris, and you notice cuts and bruises above her ankles too. You wonder if there are more. She crosses her legs. "Stop it," she says quietly.

"You have more?" You know she does. Another casualty of Alex. At least no one can see the bruises he gave you. They're hidden within your flesh.

"Did he do that?"

She looks at them closer. "Me, him, I lost track. Just penance," she says, and laughs a hollow laugh. Then she waves her hand, topic finished. She smiles. "What's up with you and my sister?" She punches you lightly on the arm.

You shrug. "I should try harder with her."

"That would be a good idea. She really likes you."

And you? Sometimes you like her; sometimes her anger is so deep, you can smell it through her pores. "I'll try."

Katie nods and kicks at the dirt with her sneakers. "I should get going. Swinging together is not helping our cause."

She gives you back your sweatshirt and you know better than to protest.

"See ya."

"Wouldn't want to be ya," you say, evoking a childish phrase that you regret as soon as the words leave your mouth.

Her face darkens and she laughs. "Ain't that the truth."

You watch her kick at the grass as she makes her way to her cottage. Then you leave, too.

Katie

He has stopped coming to me to talk. There were no picnics this summer. I tried, but he wanted to drink instead. At least he was too tired to make it up the hill to the dumpsters. Too tired to do anything but sleep, his arm around me, forgetting that I make him sick.

It's been three nights since he's come to me at all. I can't sleep. I hear a car come down the gravel path. I look out the window and see it's his. Where could he have been? Another strip club? He thinks I don't know, but I saw the matchbook peek out from his pocket.

I can do that, if that's what he wants. I can be anything. I was Pyramid Girl. I open a dresser drawer and put glitter in my hair. The voices are screaming. Ethan and Chris block the door. Tonight is my night. My terms.

I walk into the darkness.

Alex

She's waiting for me by the clothesline, just staring at the sheets blowing in the night air. Does she know I haven't been in all night? Maybe she isn't waiting for me at all, just trying to figure shit out. Like me. She likes looking at underwear on a rope and I like looking at G-strings on strippers. Same diff. But I haven't cheated. Not since we decided to try to work things out.

Strippers aren't cheating. Neither are lap dances.

I could be a complete a-hole and go to the back room, let those exotic fingers work their magic on me. But I have restraint. The most I do is pay a few bucks to cop a feel while a bitch gyrates on my lap. Then I get home and wash the skank off.

Katie turns around before I have a chance to speak. Does she smell the girls on me? Does she care? I want her to, and I don't. Sometimes she's the old Katie I knew, other times all I see is her and those guys on that video. Those times, she may as well be one of the pole girls.

"Have a fun night?" she asks. She doesn't accuse, just a regular question.

"It was all right."

She nods. "Find what you were looking for?" The way she says it gives me the creeps. She walks toward me, taking off her shirt. Her bra is purple and sheer. I don't move away, or walk to her. She moves closer, her hips gyrating. She unhooks her bra in the front and lets it fall to the wet grass.

It's past midnight, but some of the lake houses still have their lights on. "What are you doing?"

"Isn't this what you wanted?" She pushes me down on the back stoop and straddles me. Her eyes look crazy—hollow and wild at the same time.

She pulls down her pants to reveal a thong. I rip off my shirt and grab her ass. Her tits press against my chest. She pushes harder into me, putting me inside her. She moves around, clawing at my back, her eyes closed.

I'm not sure if she knows it's me she's fucking. Seems like I could be anyone. The only time she reacts is when I try to hold her. She moves her arms, wrenching free.

When we're done, she gets off and gets dressed. "How was that?"

I'm short of breath. I see my Katie. Then whore Katie. Like the thoughts of a schizo. "*What* was that?"

Her eyes focus, but only for a second. "That's not what you wanted? You like it better when the dead chickens watch?"

"Fuck you."

She laughs. "Greedy boy." Then she walks back to her cottage.

I stare after her, thoughts racing. Then, right before she opens the door, she calls out, "Don't forget to wash the skank off! Who knows where I've been."

Kyle

Two weeks go by since you first saw her bruises. You stop meeting her on the swings, but you keep watch from afar. There's something off about her. Her hair looks like straw, her clothes hang. The only times she seems strong is after flings with Alex. You don't watch those, but you know when they happen by her change in clothes—tighter, more revealing. You've also noticed she does the initiating. Her terms. You understand that—the need to be in control. But you also know when you're really not. Katie doesn't get that yet, and you're afraid she'll fall apart before she does.

You see Julie when Katie is screwing Alex. At least you know where she is at those moments. You stop bringing up Katie to Julie because that's when venom spews from Julie's lips. You have enough poison in your brain.

"So," she said the last time you saw her. The two of you were on the swings (she never goes when Katie is there), ankles touching. "Are we past everything?"

"Sure," you say.

"Good." She gets off the swing and takes your hand,

leading you to the grassy hills by the creek. She pulls you down with her onto the grass and kisses you hard and fierce. You kiss her back. Quickly, slowly, hard, soft. She gets on top of you, pulling at your clothes, taking off her shirt. You stop her before it spins out of control.

"You're right," she says, laughing. "Way too soon. Us just getting back together and all."

You kiss her again, trying the same techniques, hoping you'll feel something different than minutes ago. You don't. You're still empty. You still feel nothing. And her touch no longer makes you warm.

Julie

I know before he finally has the guts to tell me, but I make him anyway. Why should I give him an easy way out?

"It's not you," he says, our toes in the creek, moving the water around in circles.

I snort.

"It's not, Julie." Then he takes my hand, like we ever had something. Like we could still be friends. I snatch it away.

He sighs. "Don't be like that."

"Why not? If it's not me, what is it? *Who* is it? Katie?"

He stares down at his hands. I laugh. How typical. Shocker. Another boy choosing Katie. But he and I used to be friends. I go for broke. "Tell me what it is about her. Why do you all want her?" My voice cracks. I do not expect this. I brush my tears away with the back of my hand, annoyed.

"I don't want her like that." He stops, kicks at the water some more. "But I can't be with you, when things between the two of you are what they are."

She had *everything*. She *still* has Alex. Now Kyle. Why can't I at least get to feel how I do?

"What does it matter how I feel about her?" I shout. My voice floats up into the willow trees.

"It makes you ugly."

My breath flies back into me. Sharp stabs at my lungs. "Fuck you."

I jump up and pull the blanket to take it back to the lake house, but it doesn't move. I suck in air through my teeth. "Get your faggot ass off my blanket." I want to take the words back, but it's too late. Kyle rolls off in slow motion, his mind, his eyes, all of him closing me out forever.

"You know," he says, his voice emotionless I'd rather it were cold or mean because it would mean he cared—"all this time, I thought it was just Katie who needed protection. I was wrong. You need saving, too." Then he walks away.

Katie

~ The Chickens ~

Summer is almost over, and it's now or never. I won't be coming here again next year. The voices here are too loud.

Today is the last day of the chickens, and I want to watch. To see if I can. But not alone. I knock on the guys' screen door. Kyle answers, looking surprised to see me.

"It's chicken-killing day," I say.

"Hi to you too." He smiles. It's warm and safe.

"I want you to watch with me."

"God, why?"

"I want to see them today."

"Julie and Alex are already there."

His name makes me cold these days. He always enjoys their pain too much. So does she. "No, they're not the right ones for this."

He nods. "You're right. They like it too much."

Kyle closes the door of his cottage as we hear the familiar sound of tires on gravel. "You owe me."

"Big time," I say. He begins to walk to the benches, but I direct us to the bottom of the hill by the creek instead. "I don't want Julie and Kyle to see us."

His face has a question mark, but he follows me.

The chicken man brings out the first chicken. Its feathers are brownish red. It has red by its beak.

It squawks loudly. Like it's screeching. I close my eyes. Kyle squeezes my hand. "We can go. You don't have to prove anything."

My mouth is dry. "I want to see." I open my eyes again, and Chicken Man is holding a knife high in the air. It shines in the sunlight. The chicken's feather are reflected in it.

Kyle is pale.

Chicken Man swoops down with the knife and slices cleanly through the neck. I suck in air. Kyle jumps. The chicken falls at his feet immediately.

"It didn't try to fly," I say.

"What?" Kyle's voice is choked.

"Julie says they fly headless, most don't go quietly. It didn't fly."

"You need it to fly?" He's trying to understand me, but I don't even understand me.

"I don't know."

"Well, maybe the next one. But, Katie, I don't know how much more I can take."

Me neither.

Chicken Man picks up another one. Same clean slash.

It drops to his feet with a shudder as blood trickles out of its neck.

Two more. More blood. Quick and lifeless. Maybe painless.

I see Julie and Alex shake their heads and leave. Not enough of a show for them. Why did the chickens stop fighting? Maybe there was no point, since their fate wasn't going to change. They must have known. Chickens talk.

Kyle looks like he's going to throw up.

"Let's go," I say.

"You sure?" he asks.

It's nice of him to ask. I've missed nice.

"I'm sure."

We go back past the lake houses and away from the swings. Today is definitely a car-watching day.

Kyle

Night after the chicken slaughter, and you want to see her. Remembering her face—a mixture of wistfulness and empathy as she stared at the headless bodies of chickens, wanting them to fly—hurts you. Each time a new one was brought out of the cage, she squeezed your hand tightly, crushing your fingers. When the blade sliced through the neck, she let go.

Alex was on a high, hours later, scoping out the trash bin. You knew he would make her fuck him by the dumpster, and didn't understand why she let it happen. Not when she had so much control about others days they hooked up. She wasn't a chicken at the mercy of a blade. She could *really* fly away.

Tonight, you hang back behind the trees, blocking out the banging of head, arm, legs on corroded dumpster. You don't watch, just stand there in case she needs help. You hear her scream, hear Alex cursing at her to be quiet. But you don't step in to help. Only when he finishes and you're sure he's gone, do you go to her.

This time, her face is bruised. There's blood on the back

of her underwear. She crawls around on all fours picking up her clothes. When she sees you, she crawls to you. "Tell me it will be okay," she says.

You hold her naked, shivering body and tell her what she wants to hear. You cover her with your sweatshirt. She shakes against you, letting you save her. Thinking you can.

Not knowing you had the chance but chickened out.

Julie

I'm a chicken, a coward, walking around the lake houses looking for Kyle. It's become a pattern and makes me question my sanity. I want to make it look like an accident. "Oh!" I'd say after I bumped into him. "I'm sorry." I'd mumble these words and look down at my feet so he'd think I was embarrassed to have run into him after how we left things. He'd stare at me awkwardly, sigh, and finally say, "Me too." Of course, he'd mean he's sorry about how things ended, not for bumping into me. Sorry for the bigger picture. Then we'd talk, clear the air, start anew, understand each other like never before.

But I've been walking the grounds all week, and nothing. Sometimes, I run out thinking I hear his voice, but it's just a dedushka listening to the radio or a babushka watching a favorite soap. I started replaying the pretend conversation Kyle and I will have, over and over in my head, letting it lead me to where he may be. Some nights I'll stop in the middle of the gravel path and just hold my breath and listen for his footsteps. I've been thinking that maybe he's looking for me, too, and we just keep missing each other. Last night, I stood out by the lake so long my feet fell asleep.

Tonight I have a new plan. I'm going to the dumpsters since I've covered everywhere else. I'm prepared, with the nose clip I wear for diving. I walk with purpose, not scared of what I may find. I'm not a wuss like Katie.

Seems like it was a good hunch, because I hear shuffling and then whispers as I get closer. Then Kyle's voice. I speed up and stop short when I see Katie lying on the ground, naked except for Kyle's sweatshirt.

I watch them from behind a tree, my breath caught in my throat. I'm too far away to hear what they're saying, but the way he bends down protectively around her makes me sick. He helps her get dressed, and I let the anger rise up. So he doesn't see her "like that." Yeah, right. Stupid Julie, mixing up signals again.

Will Katie try to explain? Will she apologize? Give me another cardigan? Is she the innocent victim again? Poor Katie: *Why, I don't know how these things keep happening. All the boys want me, I guess.* Let her have Kyle. Mama said Katie and Kyle have the same eyes. Weak. She said I can do better than him. I think of Alex's knee on mine. All I need is time.

Alex

Idon't know who I am around her anymore, whether I'm playing a part or it's me. So I try to forget her. Picture other girls when we're fucking. Last night never happened. Went to a club tonight and grinded under the lights. The music was loud and pussy after pussy rubbed against me. This was the life. None of those bitches mattered. One dragged me outside and pushed me against the wall to blow me. I pulled at her hair. She acted like she liked it. Then she had the nerve to try to kiss me after, like I'd like the taste. I pushed her away and went to my car. "Thanks," I said, and she stuck up her middle finger at me. Stupid slut.

I get back to the cottage at one, and Katie is waiting on the back stoop. She's wearing sweats and one of those thin long-sleeved shirts that do nothing against the cold Catskill nights. She doesn't shiver, doesn't even seem to know where she is. It starts to rain.

"You lost?" I'm nothing if not funny.

She laughs quietly. "For a long time."

The rain is cold and my ass is freezing. "I'm going inside."

She nods but makes no show of moving. The rain clings to her clothes, making them look painted on. It weighs her hair down, too. I don't know the last time I really looked at her. There seems to be less to look at. Less hair. More bones. Like an anorexic in recovery. Fuck. Her face is shadowed, which is good because I don't want to see it.

I go inside, thinking she'll follow, but she doesn't move. Doesn't even seem like she's breathing. I don't need this. I go outside and pick her up. Shit, my pinkies could carry her. I lay her on my bed and back away when I see her face in the light. Makeup streaming down reveals black and blues, swelling. Fuck. I don't want to know how that happened.

She curls into a ball, spooking me out. I rummage through my drawers and find a sweatshirt and pants that will fall off her skeletal body, but they're better than what she's wearing now.

I'd tell her to take a shower and warm herself up, but the way she lies there, barely moving, I think she'd drown. Why are girls so crazy?

"Put these on," I say, tossing the dry clothes on the bed. "I'm going to make tea."

She doesn't move. Fuck, what if she took something? I don't need that on my conscience. I put on the kettle and get cookies out too. There's soft murmuring in my room and I peek in. My grandmother is stroking Katie's hair, helping her out of the soaked clothes. I walk back to the kitchen and grab the cookies and then make my way to the bedroom. My grandmother sees me and she pulls Katie close to her and waves me away, a look of disgust on her face. Why is every-thing my fault? The girl could have said no. I didn't break her.

In the kitchen, I wait until the water boils and then put the flame on low. I know I should leave, but I can't block out the glimpse I just caught of her body. Fresh cuts with trickling blood. So bony and bruised. Like a pile of broken bones. Like the carcasses.

I want her to get up. To be like those headless chickens who flew circles around my head. But she doesn't even move. Fuckin' A.

Katie

At first
I want to take pebbles with me
or water from the creek, sealed in Tupperware
I sit on the grass
and wait
for my parents to come get me
I don't know how long it is
but then
I hear their voices
from the bottom of the hill
tired, angry, annoyed
I think at me.

Julie disappeared
Ashamed
I'm sure to have more of my stench on her
Scared probably
that it would become a part of her clothes and skin
forever

A sick part of me wants Alex
Still thinks he'll look at me like he once did
I clutch the stones harder
hoping to leave their imprint on my palm
Something
to remember this place by

My father
Holds my hand tight
Like he thinks I will flee
But I chickened out long ago

There are no more Katie/Katya games to play
Neither girl wants to fight anymore

I slump low in the car seat
Up the gravel
to the highway
I think
of opening the door and jumping
to be one with the SWOOSH

I close my eyes and pretend
I'm in the small space beside the road
I venture past the line
I'm gone

Kyle

Thanks to the school calendar, your mother lets you stay an extra week at the lake house. "Lets," like you want to stay there. More like she wants the extra time for herself.

You would rather leave. It's dark here. When you ask your grandmother what happened, she pales. Says Katie looked just like your father in the last days. "Just like your father." Your grandmother mumbles the words to you, screams them to Alex. She and your grandfather walk around like your father has died all over again. Is that what will happen? Will that be Katie's fate?

Alex won't tell you what happened. Slams the door each time your grandmother mentions her name. This morning, he packed all his things and threw them into the car. Didn't even think to say good-bye to you or say he'd come back to get you.

When he leaves, your grandparents don't say good-bye to him, either. They shake their heads, faces painted in disappointment, but they seem lighter, too, once the sound of his car is no longer heard.

Julie says she knows nothing. Her grandfather finally says

you can go berry-picking with him. You are out from sunrise until noon. You speak only about the berries. When you're on your way home and the sun burns your back and the heat is causing the smell of dead, rotting flesh to waft down to the willow trees, he tells you Katie was sent away. No, not home. A place. Don't call her. Don't see her. Not for a long time.

Julie

Katie is gone. Alex is gone. Just Kyle and me, with all this opportunity to talk, and he spends the last week of summer hiding out in his cottage or throwing pebbles in the creek.

Tonight I make my move. There's nothing else to lose. "Hey," I say, forcing my mouth open, emerging from my hiding spot behind the willow tree.

He jumps. I like that I made that happen. "Hi," he says. Plop, plop, plop. For one second my heart thumps with hope. Then I remember him and Katie by the dumpster and it slows down. I wonder if it will stop beating.

Then he looks at me, searching my face for information. Of course he wouldn't be happy to see me—not unless he thought I finally had something to share with him about Katie. My heart grows icicles but I play dumb, forcing my words to drip honey. "How have you been?"

He throws a pebble from one hand to the other, like a boy just learning to juggle. "Been better." The pebble falls and he picks up another. "You?"

I smile wide, just to see his reaction. "Just fine." He takes a step back. I like that my fake cheeriness bothers him.

He turns away again and faces the water, shoulders slumping. I fight the urge to hug him. He digs up a large rock with the tip of his sandal and throws it into the water. Huge splash. "Have you heard from her?" he asks, voice low. He doesn't look at me.

I want to say, "From who?" but that's childish. Another icicle cools my heart. "She wouldn't call me." And before he can ask if maybe she called someone else, I add, "And no one tells me anything, anyway." Most likely because I show no interest. My grandmother came close to saying something once when Mama was visiting, but she stopped her. Mama wants to forget the whole thing. I heard her tell Babushka that Katie was a drama queen. Not like Julie. Julie's got a good head on her shoulders.

Kyle drops a few more pebbles into the water. He turns to face me again. "Well, if you hear from her, tell her I said hi." I see his eyes tear up and he turns away.

That's more than I can take. He never got me. Was just like Derek, falling for Katie's act. I leave him there and walk out to where my phone has a signal.

I text Alex—the one person who probably feels like me.

| Fall |

Alex

My buddy Greg tosses me a beer and turns on the tube. "Dude," he says, taking a large swig, "I don't know if I should bow to you or commit you for stupidity." He lets out a large belch of punctuation, adding fumes to the already rancid-smelling basement.

"What are you talking about?" I chug my beer and let loose my own belch that shakes the room.

"The sister conquest. One down, on to the next. How did you get around that loyalty pact sisters have?"

I clench my beer. "Wasn't an issue." *She* texted *me*. Sexted me. And I'm only human.

Greg finishes his can and does a lay-up into the trash. "That's what I'm talking about," he yells when it goes in. "Hooyah!" He high-fives me. Loser.

I flip channels until a football game comes on. The players ram into each other. Man down. He lies unmoving and I suck in air.

"Shit, that had to hurt," says Greg.

He gets back up and limps to the sidelines while the crowd applauds. I breathe again.

"You going to tap that?"

"What makes you think I haven't?" I pound another beer.

Greg laughs. "Because even you aren't that crazy. I mean, fuck, didn't her sister go psycho?"

"You don't know what you're talking about." I stare at the television.

Greg shrugs. "I know what I heard. You have some power over women."

A commercial for Fruit Loops comes on. I raise the volume.

Greg laughs. "How's that for irony?" He points to the screen. When I don't say anything, he says, "Fruit Loops. Psycho. Get it?"

"Can you just shut the fuck up?"

"Whoa, a bit touchy aren't we, Alexandra? Is it that time of the month?"

I punch him too hard on the arm and he winces in pain. "That manly enough for you?" I ask.

He puts his hands up. "Look, dude, all I'm saying is that the Julie chick is a virgin, right? If her sister has crazy genes, odds are she does, too. You can't just fuck a virgin and split. They're nuts, man. I'm not making that mistake twice. Fucking stalkers."

"Thanks for the tip." I lower the volume as the game comes on.

I feel Greg looking at me but keep my eyes on the players

slamming each other. He's not wrong, though, about the crazy part. You gotta be, right? To text the guy who put your sister in the loony bin? And what does it say about the guy who doesn't push the sister away?

Finally Greg says, "Listen, man, did you love that Katie bitch? I thought she was a skank like the rest of them. I mean, I've seen that video."

I chug another beer. "She was." Another one and another and another until I puke and everything goes black.

Katie

It's safe here. The walls are an off-yellow. One of the nurses told me it's called Antique Lace. My father has visited me a lot. My mother once. She took one look at my bruises, my broken shell, and told me to hang in there. Then she left, only to return an hour later to drop off a shampoo that was supposed to make my hair look full and shiny again. "I just bought it for Julie, and she's more beautiful than ever. You can be beautiful again, too."

"Thank you," I said, because that seemed to be what she wanted to hear. She smiled and walked out. I followed the sound of her heels growing softer and breathed out in relief when I could no longer hear them.

My father walks in now, and I'm hoping this time I can make him tell me what I want to hear.

"Hey, honey," he says, hugging me, then sitting in a plush chair across from me in the visiting room. The chair is bur-gundy. I picture the name of the color as Royal Red. "Here you go," he says, placing every tabloid magazine known to man on the table between us.

"Thank you," I say, but I mean it when I say it to him.

He smiles. "Anything new in here?"

"Same old. Therapy, painting pretty pictures of what we feel. I like it, though." Truth is, I wish I could stay here forever. No one judges me here. Not out loud. They can't.

"I'm glad, but I miss you."

I smile. "Me too."

He looks around, noticing something different each time he comes here.

"Sooo … " I say, after silence. "How's Julie?"

He tenses. "She and your mom moved out."

"Oh! I'm sorry."

He waves his hand like it's no big deal. "Don't be. I want to see your sister more, obviously, but she and your mother … they have different agendas than us."

"What do you mean?"

He shifts uncomfortably. "I don't mean anything. They're just all about appearances, that's all I meant."

I see. He looks around again. There's more. "What else?"

"Looks like the Yankees have a great shot of being in the World Series again!" He talks about baseball until my eyes glaze over.

"Have you heard from Alex?"

"I've seen him around," he says, after a pause.

"Around where?" But how is it that I already know?

My dad opens his mouth. "Katie … "

I make things easy for him. "Forget it. It's about time she

got my sloppy seconds rather than the other way around." This mean streak surprises me, but makes me feel more alive, too.

"Anger is good," he says. I think he means any emotion, happy to see me feeling something, different from the empty cask that was brought in here.

"And Kyle?"

"He's been asking to visit you. I think it will be good for you. I'm working on it with the staff."

"Thank you. How is he?"

Thing is, Kyle is a shell, too, but a walking, talking one. That time I saw his empty face when we watched the cars, I knew he was like me. I knew something was eviscerating him from the inside. He should come here before he cracks.

Julie

~Cherry Hill, NJ~

In the beginning, I was scared he'd call out *her* name while kissing me, but I shouldn't have worried. He has never mentioned her at all. It's like she never existed. I know, what kind of girl goes after her sister's ex-boyfriend, especially after everything? But no one really told me what happened, and I don't think there's a reason to make my brain work overtime to fill in the holes.

One night, after he'd left the lake houses, Alex drove back up to see me. We thought everyone was asleep, but Babushka caught us kissing in my room. She didn't flip. Didn't kick him out. Nothing. But when he left, she said, "Yulya, what are you doing? She's your *sister*."

She said that word like it meant something. Like sisters had a code, like Katie had never broken it over and over. "And?"

She shook her head. "After what he did to Katie. He's not a good person."

"I don't want to know what happened with Katie. That's not my business."

"Yulya—"

"No." I turned away. "She's not as perfect as everybody thinks. Do you know what she did? What did *he* do? Call her a whore? Maybe she needed to hear that. Maybe this time it will stick."

My grandmother's mouth set in a tight line. Color drained from her face. Then she walked away.

But not Mama.

When Alex visited me in Cherry Hill, Dad yelled, told him to get the hell out of our house. Not Mama. Surprisingly, she was the only one who supported me. It's like I can do no wrong. Dad stormed out, but Mama told Alex to come into our kitchen. She talked to him. To *me*. That night, she brushed my hair and braided it. The next day, we went shopping and bought me new, pretty clothes. The kind she only bought for Katie before. She told me to spin around in the mirror. She said she was impressed that I'd hooked such a good-looking guy. He had nothing on Kyle, she said, laughing. I laughed with her. She told me she liked it when Alex was around because he made her feel young and alive. I get that. Chloe *died* when I showed her his pic. The cheerleaders told me I needed to try out, like, "for realz." Now that Marissa and Katie are both gone, they "like so need a new Pyramid Girl."

Mama told me not to do anything stupid. I only get one shot.

Tomorrow, Mama is throwing a house-warming party at

our new apartment. She's inviting all her fancy friends and told me to invite mine. She wants to show Alex off, she said. Show *me* off. It's funny how things work out.

Kyle

When you get there, she hugs you tight and doesn't let go. Then she steps back and examines you. "You look the same," she says, almost disappointed.

"Sorry."

She shakes her head and smiles. "I just, I don't know. Somehow I expected you to look different. I *feel* different. Dad looked different."

You smile back. "I'm the same."

"Hmm," she says, thinking this over, then nods.

You grab a chair and move it beside her bed. That's where she's sitting. "So what's been going on?" You want to talk to her like everything is normal, has always been.

"Well, as you can see, we're in my room. That's a *biiiig* deal. They trust me to be by myself with someone from the"—she drops her voice to a whisper—"outside."

"And I'm the first to visit you under these new conditions? I'm honored."

"You should be."

"Does that mean you're closer to getting out? Can I spring you?"

"Nah, it's good here. I'm staying here forever and forever." She singsongs the last part, but you don't think she's kidding. "Want to join me?"

Not that you haven't thought about it. You've been thinking too much lately. Jasmine has come around, always after his shifts. Always when you're supposed to be asleep. Even Alex won't rouse you from your sleep. But he *has* started hinting about you joining him and Julie. You laugh it off, like you think he's kidding. But he's getting more insistent. And you don't understand. He's not the same Alex. Some days he doesn't get out of bed. Some nights he wakes up screaming Katie's name. He walks around like he thinks her ghost will jump out and make him feel again, but can you call someone a ghost if they only died on the inside? And then you get it. He's trying to get the old Alex back. The pre-Katie Alex. But he's gone, roaming the grounds with pre-Alex Katie.

"Aaah," says Katie smiling. "You *have* thought about it."

You shrug. She gets off the bed and walks to the door, looking in one direction then the other. Satisfied, she closes the door and walks back to you.

"Let me show you what we do here," she says, reaching under the mattress. She takes out a stack of drawing paper. "They want me to make pretty pictures and sometimes I do, but when no one is looking, I make these."

She hands them to you. You look at the sketches of mutilated chickens. Some with blood dripping from their feet. Others from their wings. All headless.

"This is you getting better?" And here you thought this place could help you.

She smiles. "No. That was in the beginning. On my bad days, I draw some more. But I still have to keep them hidden because they wouldn't get it."

She reaches under the other side of the mattress. "This," she says, "is what I've been drawing this week."

When you don't move to get them, she plops them onto your lap. At first you don't want to look.

"Come on," she says. "Don't be a chicken."

You laugh and look at the pictures. These chickens don't have heads, but they have feathers. Their feet aren't bleeding. The last one is whole, wings up in flight, stitches around its neck.

Kyle

How is she?" your mother asks when you get home.
"Getting better," you say.

"Good," she says, but her mind is somewhere else.

You look at the clock. She should have been at work thirty minutes ago. You see her stockings on the chair beside her.

"You not going in today?" you say.

"It's my fault," she says.

"What is?" There are so many answers to this question.

"Alex. You were little; you may not remember. I had all those men."

"I wasn't that little. I remember."

She puts her face in her hands. "We needed the money. I looked away too many times. They beat him up."

You don't remember this. How could you not have known?

"I remember some of them hit *you*," you say.

She nods. "And him."

Where were *you*? Why didn't they hit *you*? Did Alex serve himself up instead?

"And me?" you ask.

She shrugs. "You were my baby. I protected you more."

You don't know what to say to this. She didn't protect you enough.

"I messed up," she says. "I should have saved you both."

You blink at her. "You didn't save me," you say.

She blinks back, confused. "You mean your father? He was a sick man. I've apologized over and over for what happened with him."

You see how old she's gotten. How deep the creases near her eyes are. The lines around her mouth. But you need to tell her or you will drown. "No," you say. "You didn't save me."

Then you tell her. About the first time with Alex and GDJ. About the others. About the bruises inside you no one can see.

She cries when you finish. Moves to hold you, but moves back unsure. "I'm sorry," she says again. "I'm so sorry."

Then she gets up and goes to the phone. "Julie is only fifteen, right?"

You nod.

She dials. A last attempt at saving someone.

Kyle

You are Katie's plus-one to the Treatment Center's Halloween bash. You go as a cowboy. Because you get to wear jeans and it reminds you of Wild West City. The gazebo outside is strung with black and orange lights. There is a band playing "Monster Mash." They even set up a dimly lit haunted walk. Katie has seen none of it yet.

She's bouncy when she sees you. Excited, happy. She's dressed as a cheerleader. It's symbolic, she says. That she's owning all of herself. Past and present. She hasn't gained back all the weight, and the skirt hangs slightly below her hips. Her still-too-thin hair is tied back with a ribbon. But her eyes are alive and fuller than you've seen in a long time. You tell her she looks beautiful.

She laughs when you say that. "I told you this place was magic."

You stop in her room on the way to the party. She shows you more stitched-up chickens.

"You better not let them see these or they'll think you're all healed," you say.

"Wouldn't dream of it." The loudspeakers request that all residents and guests go to the gazebo.

"Before we go," she says, reaching into a drawer, "I have something to give you."

She gives you a stack of pamphlets about the Center. About asking for help.

You—

I.

You—

I.

I.

I.

I put the pamphlets in my satchel and take Katie's hand. We walk through the double-glass doors. Through the darkness, into the lights.

Resources

Sometimes, we don't speak up because we're afraid. Other times, it's because we feel what's happening is the norm or that we deserve the pain inflicted. But no one does. Below are resources to contact if you have been a victim of digital or sexual abuse or part of an abusive relationship. The list also includes networks where you can connect to others in the same situation, both virtually and in person.

Digital abuse, according to a 2009 study conducted by the AP and MTV, is "writing something online that wasn't true, sharing information that a person didn't want shared, writing something mean, spreading false rumors, threatening physical harm, impersonation, spying, posting embarrassing photos or video, being pressured to send naked photos, being teased, and encouraging people to hurt themselves" (*CNET News*, 12/3/09). If you or someone you know has been a victim, you will find the sites listed below helpful:

- **That's Not Cool (www.thatsnotcool.com)**
  This site focuses on all areas of digital abuse. It also provides information on standing up to the bullying, additional resources, and the opportunity to chat with others who have been digitally abused.

- **A Thin Line (www.athinline.org)**
  MTV's *A Thin Line* campaign was "developed to empower teens to identify, respond to, and stop the spread of digital abuse in their life and amongst their peers." The site provides information on where to get help and what to do if you're being digitally abused, and

encourages sharing your story and getting involved in stopping digital abuse.

- **Wired Safety (www.wiredsafety.org)**
Wired Safety is an online safety and help group. It has information on a variety of digital abuse, including sexting, sextortion, and cyberbullying, and what to do if you or someone you know is a victim. By May 2012, they will offer a teen hotline staffed by teens who provide assistance.

If you or someone you know has been *sexually abused*:

- **RAINN: Rape, Abuse, and Incest, National Network (www.rainn.org)**
RAINN is the nation's largest anti–sexual assault organization. Call the hotline at 1-800-656-HOPE or visit the online hotline at https://ohl.rainn.org/online/.

- **After Silence (www.aftersilence.org)**
After Silence provides support for rape, sexual assault, and sexual abuse survivors via message boards and chatrooms.

- **Pandora's Project (www.pandorasaquarium.org)**
The mission of Pandora's Project is to "provide information, facilitate peer support and offer assistance to male and female survivors of sexual violence and their friends and family" via an online support group, message board, and chatroom for rape and sexual abuse survivors. It also offers a Sexual Assault Lending Library, which lends materials on sexual violence and recovery, free of charge.

- **Male Survivor: National Organization Against Male Sexual Victimization** (www.malesurvivor.org) Information and referrals for male survivors of sexual assault and the professionals working with them. There are referrals to local resources and a discussion board, chatroom, newsletter, and online bulletin board.

If you or someone you know is in an *abusive dating relationship*:

- **Loveisrespect** (www.loveisrespect.org) Loveisrespect, a national 24-hour resource that can be accessed online or by phone (1-866-331-9474 & 1-866-331-8453 TTY) is specifically designed for teens and young adults. The helpline and online chat offer real-time, one-on-one support from trained Peer Advocates. There are also quizzes and information on what to do about dating rumors, how to determine if you are in an abusive relationship, etc.

- **The National Center for Victims of Crime The Dating Violence Resource Center** (http://www.ncvc.org/ncvc/main.aspx?dbID=DB_Dating ViolenceResourceCenter101) portion of this site provides information on how to determine if a relationship is abusive and how to seek help if you or someone you know is in an abusive relationship, along with a hotline and additional resources (like how to create your own teen outreach project to raise dating violence awareness).

- **The National Coalition of Anti-Violence Programs (NCAVP) (www.ncavp.org/AVPs/default.aspx)**
  The NCAVP is a "coalition of programs that document and advocate for victims of anti-LGBT and anti-HIV/AIDS violence/harassment, domestic violence, sexual assault, police misconduct and other forms of victimization." The site addresses a variety of violence issues against the LGBT community and also provides a comprehensive list of local anti-violence organizations to contact for help.

Photo by Samuel Peltz

About the Author

Margie Gelbwasser's debut YA novel, *Inconvenient*, published by Flux in 2010, was named a 2011 Sydney Taylor Notable Book for Teens. When not writing about secrets in suburbia, she likes cooking, hiking, and being with her husband and four-year-old son. Visit her online at www.margiewrites.com.